"How old are you?" Matthew asked suddenly.

"Does it matter?"

He inclined his head. "Humor me."

Helen hesitated. "Twenty-two." Then, with some dignity, "As you've got what you came for, can I get up?"

Her words irritated him more than a little but he contained his anger and said quietly, "So, how did you get to the age of twenty-two without—without—"

Matthew couldn't find the right words, but in the event he didn't need to. "Just unlucky, I guess," Helen responded, with obvious sarcasm.

He sighed. "It's incredible!"

ANNE MATHER began writing when she was a child, progressing through torrid teenage romances to the kind of adult romances she likes to read. She's married, and lives in the north of England. After writing, she enjoys reading, driving and traveling to different places to find settings for new novels. She considers herself very lucky to do something that she not only enjoys, but also gets paid for.

Books by Anne Mather

HARLEQUIN PRESENTS

Anne Mather

A Woman of Passion

Harlequin Books

TORONTO • NEW YORK • LONDON
AMSTERDAM • PARIS • SYDNEY • HAMBURG
STOCKHOLM • ATHENS • TOKYO • MILAN
MADRID • WARSAW • BUDAPEST • AUCKLAND

ISBN 0-373-11797-3

A WOMAN OF PASSION

First North American Publication 1996.

Printed in U.S.A.

CHAPTER ONE

THE man was there again. Helen could see him striding away along the shoreline, the creamy waves lapping the soles of his canvas boots. It was almost impossible to make out any distinguishing features from this distance, but he was tall and dark-haired, and the way he walked made her think he was not seeking recognition. On the contrary, if she was an imaginative female—which she'd always assured herself she wasn't—she'd have speculated that he took his walk so early to avoid meeting anyone.

She had no idea who he was. And doubted that if she'd observed him at any other time of the day he'd have aroused any interest at all. But for the past three mornings—ever since her arrival, in fact—she had seen him walking the beach at six a.m. Always alone, and always too far away for her to identify him.

Of course, if she herself had not been suffering the effects of the time-change between London and Barbados, she probably wouldn't have been awake at six a.m. But, as yet, her metabolism hadn't adapted to a five-hour time-lag, and each morning she'd found herself leaning on her balcony rail, waiting for the sun to make its appearance.

And it was probably just as well that the man chose to walk along the shoreline, she reflected ruefully. Standing here, in only the thin cotton shift she wore to sleep in, she would not have liked to think herself observed. At this hour of the morning, when no one else in the villa was awake, she could enjoy the beauty of her surroundings unhindered. Once the children were awake—and Tricia—her time was no longer her own.

Yet she shouldn't complain, she told herself severely. Without Tricia's help, she had no idea what she'd have done. A young woman of twenty-two, with no particular skills or talents, was anathema. Would-be employers wanted written qualifications, not heartfelt assurances that she could do the job they had to offer.

Of course, until her father's untimely death, she hadn't given a lot of thought to earning her own living. She'd been reasonably well educated, though she'd be the first to admit she was no academic. Nevertheless, she had attended an exclusive girls' school and an equally exclusive finishing-school in Switzerland, and she'd considered herself admirably suited to maintain her role in life.

Which had been what? She pulled a wry face now. Well, to find a man like her father, she supposed—or like the man she had thought her father to be—and get married, raise a family, and repeat the process with her own children.

She sighed. Only it wasn't to be. She wondered if her father had given any thought to her dilemma when he'd taken his yacht out for the last time. Had he really jumped, or had he only fallen? With the sea calm and the yacht found drifting, unmanned, ten miles south of the Needles, it was hard not to think the worst.

Naturally, she had been distraught when they brought her the news. She couldn't believe that her father, who had been an excellent yachtsman, could actually have drowned. And the fact that they'd not found his body had kept her hopes alive. Whatever the coastguards said, he wasn't dead.

But he was. His body had been found a couple of days later, and the realisation that she was alone now had been numbing. Even at the funeral she'd half expected James Gregory to come striding into the chapel. It was strange how that had sustained her through all the interminable expressions of grief.

Afterwards, however, while the guests were making a rather unsympathetic attack on the splendid buffet the housekeeper had provided, Max Thomas, her father's solicitor, had drawn her aside. And in a few short words he had swept the ground from under her feet. Her father, it appeared, had been destitute. For years he'd been living on borrowed time, and now that time had run out.

Incredibly, considering the affluent lifestyle they had enjoyed, James Gregory had been in serious financial difficulties. The estate he'd inherited from his father— and which had supported successive generations of Gregorys—was bankrupt. In spite of the pleas of his tenants for an injection of capital, no help had been offered. And, although a couple of years ago he had had the idea of opening the house and grounds to the public, that too had proved unsuccessful without the proper investment.

Remembering all those holidays in the Caribbean, the winters spent in Gstaad, the summers in the South of France, Helen had had no doubt as to how her father had spent his money. And he'd never betrayed his anxieties to her. She'd always had everything she'd ever wanted.

Maybe if her mother had still been around things would have been different. There was no doubt that Fleur Gregory's departure, when Helen had been barely four years old, had had a salutary effect on her father. Until then he'd seemed quite content to live in the country. But her mother had found country life boring, and she'd eventually run off with a wealthy polo-player from Florida she'd met at a party in town.

That was when James Gregory had bought the London apartment, but, from Helen's point of view, living in London had seemed rather boring at first. She had missed her friends, and she had missed the horses, and although they continued to spend holidays at Conyers it had never been quite the same.

Of course as she'd got older and started school her attitudes had changed. Her friends had been in London then. They had been young people from a similar background. And the boyfriends she'd eventually collected had all been as fun-loving as her father.

But her father had only been what she had made him, she reflected sadly, remembering how devastated she'd been to learn that her father had been borrowing money on the strength of securities he no longer owned. The estate had not one, but three mortgages hanging over it, and with the interest that was owing and death duties, there'd been precious little left.

The following months had been harrowing. Coming to terms with her father's death would have been bad enough; coming to terms with the fact of his probable suicide had been infinitely worse.

Everything had had to be sold, even her car and the little jewellery she'd owned, and because her father's only living relative was an elderly aunt, who'd disowned him long ago, Helen had had to deal with all the awful details herself. Max Thomas had helped, but even he had had no idea how distressing it had been. People who had once professed themselves her father's friends had cut her dead in the street. Young men who'd phoned her constantly had suddenly been out of reach.

Not that Helen had particularly cared about her sudden loss of status. The hardest thing to bear was the absence of the one person she had really loved. She didn't blame her father for what he'd done, but she did miss him. And she wished he had confided in her before taking that final step.

She could have contacted her mother's sister, she supposed. Aunt Iris must have read about what had happened in the newspapers, but she hadn't been in touch. Besides, Helen had shied away from the idea of asking for charity from the Warners. She and her father had had nothing to do with them in recent years, and it would have been hypocritical to ask for help now.

Nevertheless, things had been fairly desperate when she'd run into Tricia Sheridan in Marks & Spencer's. In the four months since her father died she hadn't been able to find a job, and although she had only been living in a bed-sitter, the rent had still to be paid. Office managers, store managers—all wanted more than the paltry qualifications she had to offer. The only position that had been open to her was a forecourt attendant at a petrol station, and she had been seriously thinking of taking it when Tricia came along.

Tricia, whose husband worked for the Foreign Office, had been living in Singapore for the past two years. She was older than Helen; she had been a prefect when Helen was still in middle school, but because of her prowess at sports all the younger girls had admired her.

She had singled Helen out for attention because Helen's father had presented the school with a new gymnasium. A gymnasium he couldn't afford, Helen reflected sadly now. But at the time she'd been so proud of his generosity.

Tricia had quickly discerned Helen's situation. And had been quick to offer assistance. Why didn't Helen come to work for her? she'd suggested. She needed a nanny, and she was sure Helen could cope.

It had all happened so quickly that Helen hadn't really stopped to ask herself why—if five-year-old Henry and four-year-old Sophie were such poppets—Tricia didn't have a nanny already. The other woman's explanation that as they had been out of the country for some time they were out of touch with current agencies, hadn't really held water, when she'd had time to think about it. She'd simply been so relieved to be offered a job that she'd agreed to her terms without question.

She supposed she'd had some naïve idea that there were still people in the world who did do things out of the kindness of their hearts. Even after all the awful experiences she'd had, she'd actually been prepared to take Tricia's offer at face value. She needed a job; Tricia was offering one. And the salary was considerably larger than any she'd been offered thus far.

In addition to which she would not have to pay the rent on the bed-sitter. Naturally, Tricia had declared, she must live in. Nannies always lived in, she'd said. It was one of the advantages of the job.

Helen wondered now whether she would have stuck it as long as she had if she had not given up her bed-sit. In a short time she'd discovered that, far from being out of touch with the agencies, Tricia had, in fact, tried several before offering the post to her. Unfortunately, her requirements did not jell with most modern-day nannies. They were either too old, or too flighty, or they couldn't follow orders, she'd declared, when Helen had mentioned her findings. But Helen had a theory that they simply refused to be treated as servants.

In any event, beggars couldn't be choosers, and in the three months since she'd been working for the Sheridans, Helen had discovered it wasn't all bad. Tricia was selfish and demanding, and she did expect the younger woman to turn her hand to anything if required. But, when their mother wasn't around to encourage them, Henry and Sophie were fun to be with, and Andrew Sheridan was really rather nice.

Not that he was around much, Helen conceded, cupping her chin on her hand and watching the man who had started her introspection disappear into the belt of palms that fringed the far end of the beach. His work took him away a lot, which might have some bearing on Tricia's uncertain temper. That, and the fact that he never seemed to take her seriously. As easy-going as he was, Helen could quite see how frustrating it must be to try and sustain his attention.

For herself, she imagined a lot of people would consider her position a sinecure. After all, she had her own room, she was fed and watered regularly, and the salary she was earning meant she could put a considerable amount each month into her savings account. If her hours were long, and a little erratic, she had nothing else to do. And at least Tricia didn't feel sorry for her, even if she could be a little patronising at times.

Still, she wouldn't be here if it wasn't for Tricia, she reminded herself firmly, lifting her face to the first silvery rays of sunlight that swept along the shoreline. The fine sand, which until then had had an opalescent sheen, now warmed to palest amber, and the ocean's depths glinted with a fragile turquoise light. Colours that had been muted lightened, and a breeze brushed her calves beneath her muslin hem.

It was all incredibly beautiful, and the temptation was to linger, and enjoy the strengthening warmth of the sun. Helen felt as if she could watch the constant movement of the waves forever. There was a timelessness about them that soothed her nerves and renewed her sense of worth.

But she had spent quite long enough thinking about the past, she decided. Turning back into her bedroom, she viewed her tumbled bed with some remorse. It would have been so easy to crawl back into its comfort. Why was it she felt sleepy now, when an hour ago she couldn't rest?

The room, like all the rooms in the villa Tricia had rented, was simply furnished: a bed, a couple of rattan chairs, a chest of drawers. There was a fitted wardrobe between this room and its adjoining bathroom, and louvred shutters on the windows to keep it cool. The bedrooms weren't air-conditioned, even though Tricia had kicked up something of a fuss when she'd discovered this. However, the maid who looked after the villa had remained impassive. There was nothing she could do about it, she said. Perhaps the lady would prefer to stay at the hotel?

Tricia hadn't preferred. It was far too convenient to have their own place with their own kitchen, where Henry and Sophie could take their meals without constant supervision. In addition to which, the place belonged to a business friend of Andrew's. And he would not be amenable to them transferring to an hotel.

As she took her shower—tepid water, but refreshing—Helen remembered that Tricia's husband was joining them today. He hadn't accompanied them out to the Caribbean. Tricia had explained that there were meetings he had to attend, but Helen suspected Andrew had simply wanted to avoid such a long journey with two demanding children. As it was, she had had to spend most of the flight playing card games with Henry. Tricia and Sophie had fallen asleep, but Henry had refused to close his eyes.

Still, they were here now, and for the next four weeks surely she could relax and enjoy the sun. She'd already discovered that it was easier entertaining her young charges when the beach was on their doorstep. So long as Tricia didn't get bored, and insist on giving parties every night.

The shower left her feeling refreshed and decidedly more optimistic, and after straightening the sheets on the bed she pulled on cotton shorts, which were all she wore over her bikini. It had been Tricia's suggestion that she dress like one of the family. Any attempt to dress formally here would have seemed foolish.

It was only a little after half-past six when Helen emerged from the villa and crossed the terrace. Her feet were bare, and she took care not to stand on any of the prostrate beetles, lying on their backs on the tiles. These flying beetles mostly appeared at night, attracted by the artificial light, and, although she knew they were harmless, Helen had still to get used to their size and speed of movement. She had a horror of finding one in her bed, and she was always glad when Maria, the maid, brought out her broom and swept them away.

Beyond the terrace, a stretch of grass and a low stone wall was all that separated the grounds of the villa from the beach. Although she would have liked to go for a walk along the beach herself, Helen knew the children would be getting up soon and demanding her attention. It was no use expecting Maria to keep an eye on them when she arrived to prepare breakfast. Likeable though she was, she was also lazy, and looking after infants was not her job.

Perching on the wall, Helen drew one leg up to her chin and wrapped her arms around it. The sun was definitely gaining in strength, and she could feel its heat upon her bare shoulders. Although her skin seldom burned, she had taken to wearing a screening cream this holiday. The sun had a definite edge to it these days, and she had no wish to risk its dangers.

All the same, it was amazing to think that the temperature in England was barely above freezing. When they had left London three days ago, it had actually been snowing. But February here was one of the nicest months of the year. There was little of the humidity that built up later on.

The water beyond the beach was dazzling. It was tinged with gold now, its blue-green brilliance reflective as it surged towards the shore. Helen had already found that its power could sweep an unwary bather from her feet. Its smoothness was deceptive, and she had learned to be wary.

Fortunately, there was a shallow pool in the grounds of the villa where the youngsters could practise their strokes. They'd both learned to swim while they were living in Singapore, and although their skills were limited they could safely stay afloat. Helen had spent most of yesterday morning playing with them in the pool. Tricia had gone into Bridgetown, to look up some old friends.

'Helen!'

Henry's distinctive call interrupted her reverie, and, turning her head, she saw both children standing on the veranda, waving at her. They were still in their pyjamas, and she got resignedly to her feet. Until it was time for their afternoon nap, Tricia expected her to take control.

'Have you been for a swim?' asked Sophie resentfully, as Helen walked along the veranda to their room. She pointed at the damp braid of streaked blonde hair that lay over one shoulder. 'You should've waked us. We could have come with you.'

'Woken us,' said Helen automatically, realising as she did so how quickly she had fallen into the role of nursemaid. 'And, no. I haven't been for a swim, as it happens.' She shooed them back into their bedroom. 'I had a shower, that's all. That's why my hair is wet.'

'Why didn't you dry it?' began Sophie, then Henry turned on his little sister.

'For God's sake,' he exclaimed, 'give it a rest, can't you?' He flushed at Helen's reproving stare. 'Well—she's such a stupid girl.'

'I'm not stupid!'

Sophie responded loudly enough, but her eyes had filled with tears. She always came off worst in any argument with her brother, and although she tried to be his equal she usually lost the battle.

'I don't think this conversation is getting us anywhere, do you?' declared Helen smoothly. 'And, Henry—if you want to make a statement, kindly do so without taking God's name in vain.'

'Mummy does,' he muttered, though he'd expected Helen's reproof. 'In any case, I'm hungry. Has Maria started breakfast?'

'I doubt it.' Helen started the shower as the two children began to unbutton their pyjamas. 'She hasn't arrived yet, as far as I know.'

'Not arrived?' Henry sounded horrified. 'But I want something to eat.'

'Then we'll have to see what she's left in the fridge,' said Helen calmly. 'Now, come on, Sophie. You're first.'

By the time the children were bathed and dressed, Helen had already refereed a dozen arguments. Anyone who thought having children of a similar age automatically meant they would be company for one another couldn't be more wrong, Helen reflected drily. In some circumstances it might work, and she was prepared to accept that there must be exceptions, but Henry and Sophie were in constant competition, and it didn't make for amiable dispositions.

To her relief, Maria had arrived and was making the morning's batch of rolls, when they arrived in the kitchen in search of breakfast. 'Morning, Miss Gregory,' she greeted Helen with a smile. 'You're up and about very early.'

'I guess it's because I still haven't got used to the fact that it's not lunchtime already,' replied Helen. She rubbed her flat stomach with a rueful hand. 'It's the hunger that does it. We're all ravenous!'

'Well, sit down, sit down. I've a batch of rolls in the oven that's almost ready. Why don't you have some orange juice, while you're waiting? Or there's some grapefruit in the fridge, if you'd prefer it.'

'I don't want grapefruit,' said Sophie, wrinkling her nose, but Henry only looked at her with contempt.

'I do,' he declared, though Helen knew he didn't like it. 'You're just a baby. You still drink milk.'

'I drink milk, too,' said Helen firmly, before it could deteriorate into another argument. 'Would you like orange juice, Sophie? That's what I'm going to have.'

'Mmm,' Sophie was off-hand, until she saw her brother's face when Helen put half a grapefruit in front of him. Then she gave him a mocking smirk, and sipped her juice with exaggerated enjoyment.

Helen was helping herself to a second cup of coffee when Tricia appeared in the kitchen doorway. She wasn't dressed yet. She was wearing a trailing chiffon négligé, and her reddish hair hadn't been combed and stood out around her head. A tall woman, whose adolescent athleticism hadn't continued into adulthood, Tricia had a constant battle to remain slim. It was a fact that she resented and which caused her some irritation. She regarded the little group around the table now without liking, and when Sophie would have slid off her chair and run to greet her mother she waved her back.

'D'you have any aspirin, Maria?' she asked, with a weary tilt of her head. 'I've got the most God-awful headache. It must have been that seafood you served us last night. Are you sure it was fresh?'

It was hardly the way to gain Maria's sympathy, and before the woman could make any comment, Helen pushed back her chair. 'I've got some paracetamol,' she offered. 'It's good for headaches.' Particularly hangovers, she added silently, recalling how Tricia had drunk the best part of two bottles of wine the night before.

'Oh, have you?' Tricia turned to her with some relief. 'D'you think you could bring them to my room? I think I'll stay in bed this morning.'

'But you said you'd take us into town this morning,' Henry protested, not yet old enough to know when to keep his mouth shut, and his mother turned on him angrily.

'What a selfish boy you are!' she exclaimed. 'Always thinking of yourself. Perhaps you'd like to spend the morning in bed as well. It might make you realise I'm not doing it for fun.'

'Oh, Mummy——'

'I don't think Henry meant to upset you,' put in Helen hurriedly, earning a grateful look from her young charge. 'Why don't you go back to bed, as you say, Tricia? I'll get the paracetamol, and then bring your breakfast on a tray. I'm sure you could manage a croissant, and Maria's brought some mango jelly and it's delicious.'

'Well...' Tricia adopted a petulant air. 'That does sound nice, Helen, but I don't know if I'll be able to eat anything. My head's throbbing, and I'm sure I'm running a temperature. I may have to call the doctor if it doesn't let up soon.'

'I'm sorry.'

Helen could sympathise with her. Having a headache in a hot climate always seemed so much worse. The light was so bright, for one thing, and there seemed no escape from the heat.

Tricia sighed. 'Perhaps if you brought me some coffee?' she suggested. 'And a little orange juice to wash the tablets down. Oh—and maybe a lightly boiled egg, hmm? And do you think you could find a slice of toast?'

'Leave it to me.'

Helen ushered the other woman out of the room, before she could remember the threat she'd made to Henry. Then, when Tricia was safely installed in her bedroom, she returned to the kitchen to find Maria grinning broadly.

'Just a lightly boiled egg,' she declared wryly. 'And some coffee and some orange juice and some toast...' She paused to give Helen a wink. 'Did I miss something?'

Helen wouldn't let herself be drawn. All the same, it wasn't the first time Tricia had spent the morning in bed. When they were in London, she had seldom seen her employer before lunchtime. If Tricia wasn't attending some function or other, she rarely got up before noon.

When the tray was prepared, she collected the paracetamol from her room and delivered it in person. Tricia was lying back against the pillows, shading her eyes with a languid wrist, which she removed when Helen came into the room.

'Oh, there you are,' she said. 'What have you been doing? I've been waiting ages.'

'Just five minutes,' Helen assured her, depositing the legs of the tray across her knees. 'Now, if you want me, I'll be on the beach. I'm going to take the children to search for shells.'

Tricia shuffled into a sitting position, and reached for the orange juice. 'Well, don't be long,' she said, swallowing the tablets Helen had given her with a mouthful of the juice. 'You're going to have to go and pick Drew up from the airport. I can't possibly do it. His plane is due in just after two.'

Helen stared at her. 'But that's this afternoon. You'll probably be feeling perfectly all right by then.'

'I won't. I never feel all right until the evening,' replied Tricia firmly. 'And driving all that way in these conditions—well, it's simply out of the question.'

Helen took a breath. 'He'll be expecting you to pick him up,' she said carefully.

'Then he'll be disappointed, won't he?' Tricia regarded her testily. 'My God, you're almost as bad as Henry. Does no one care that I've got a migraine? I can't help it if I'm not well.'

'No.' Helen moistened her lips. She'd already learned that there was no point in arguing with Tricia when she was in this mood. 'Well—will you take care of Sophie and Henry, then? I don't think Maria is willing——'

'Can't they go with you?'

Tricia stared at her impatiently, and Helen realised she wasn't being given a choice. She couldn't leave the children to look after themselves. But it was almost an hour to the airport, and Sophie, particularly, didn't travel well.

'Can we leave it until nearer lunchtime?' she suggested, hoping against hope that Tricia might have changed her mind by then. She'd have thought her employer would have been keen to see her husband again. It was several days since they'd come away.

'I expect you to go and meet Drew,' Tricia informed her inflexibly, and Helen couldn't help thinking that there was no sign of the frail invalid they had encountered earlier. 'Must I remind you that if it wasn't for me you might not have a job? Let alone a well-paid one in enviable surroundings.'

'No.' Helen felt her colour deepen. 'I mean—yes. Yes, I do appreciate it.' She turned towards the door. 'I'll—tell the children.'

'Good.' Tricia attacked her egg with evident enthusiasm. 'Just so long as we understand one another, Helen. I don't like pulling rank here, but it really had to be said.'

CHAPTER TWO

MATTHEW AITKEN lounged behind the wheel of the dust-smeared Range Rover, waiting for his assistant, Lucas Cord, to emerge from the arrivals hall. He was getting impatient. The plane from New York had landed more than twenty minutes ago, and as Fleur had been booked into a first-class seat her luggage should have been cleared some time ago.

It was hot where he was sitting. There was little shade at this time of day and, despite the air-conditioning in the vehicle, which had been working fairly adequately on the journey to the airport, a prolonged period of waiting was causing the heat to rise. The annoying thing was that he wouldn't have been here at all if his phone hadn't been out of order. He'd discovered that when he'd tried to call New York that morning, and as he needed to speak to his publisher rather urgently he'd had no choice but to try elsewhere.

In consequence, it had made sense to continue on to the airport. Lucas had offered to make the call for him, but he'd wanted to speak to Marilyn himself. It was so much easier to deal with the matter personally. And the delay in the completion of the manuscript was his problem.

All the same, he disliked giving Fleur the impression that he had nothing better to do than come and meet her. It wasn't as if he was even eager to have her here. But she was still his sister-in-law, even if his brother was no longer around. Chase's death at the age of forty-two had been such a bitter blow.

Which, of course, was why the latest manuscript hadn't been completed. Although it was eight weeks now since Chase's fall, he was finding it hard to work.

Dammit, he thought irritably, what had Chase been thinking of to attack his opponent so recklessly? It wasn't as if he was an amateur. He'd been playing polo for almost thirty years.

Fleur, of course, had been devastated. When he'd seen her at the funeral, he hadn't doubted that it was a blow to her, too. She had been dressed all in black and oozing tears, and he'd had to feel sympathy for her. For the first time in his life, he'd pitied her. He couldn't believe even she could have wanted Chase dead.

But as he sat there in the Range Rover, with sweat dampening the shirt on his back and his bare thighs sticking to the leather seat, he couldn't help remembering that he hadn't always felt so charitably towards her. He'd been only sixteen when his brother had brought Fleur to live with them. The fact that she had still been married to her first husband at that time hadn't sat too happily with their father either, but Chase had been mad about her, and somehow they'd all settled down.

It was just as well his own mother hadn't been around, Matthew reflected drily. Emily Aitken had died of a rare form of cancer when he was ten, and until Fleur had come to live at the ranch their housekeeper, Rosa Cortez, had been both wife and mother to the three men.

Fleur had changed all that. In no time at all she was giving Rosa orders, telling his father what to do, and bullying Chase into doing whatever she wanted. His father hadn't liked it but he was a mild man, more at home with temperamental horses than temperamental women, and at least he could escape into the stables whenever he felt like it.

Of course, the horses their father bred were what had enabled Chase to become the successful sportsman he had been. The Aitken Stud was famous throughout the United States, and enthusiasts came from as far afield as Argentina and Europe to buy the spirited stallions he produced. It was a lucrative business, and for all Matthew had been so young, he had had no doubt that Chase's wealth had been a goodly part of his allure. Fleur had liked spending his money too much to have been attracted to a poor man, and he'd sometimes wondered what her first husband must have been like, and whether he had been wealthy, too.

Fortunately, during the early years of their marriage, he, Matthew, had spent most of his time away. College, and then university, had enabled him to avoid the image of his big brother being turned from a laughing, confident man into a grovelling supplicant. Whatever Fleur had, Chase had certainly been hooked on it, and Matthew had preferred to stay out of their way whenever he was at home.

He had been twenty-two when Fleur tried to seduce him. He remembered the occasion vividly. Chase had been away, playing a match in Buenos Aires, and his father had been attending the horse sales in Kentucky. Matthew wouldn't have been there at all had it not been for the fact that he was attending an interview the following day in Tallahassee. The editor of the *Tallahassee Chronicle* was looking for a junior reporter, and Matthew had been hoping to get the job.

At first he hadn't believed what was happening. When Fleur had come to his room, he'd assumed there really must be something wrong. It was when she had complained of being so lonely and started to shed her satin wrap that he'd comprehended. And, although his hot young body had been burning, he'd succeeded in throwing her out.

However, he hadn't been able to hide the fact that she'd aroused him, and Fleur had seen his weakness as a challenge. At every opportunity she'd let him see how willing she was to be with him, touching him with clinging hands, bestowing longing looks.

Matthew had been sickened by it. It wasn't as if there had been any shortage of women his own age, ready and willing to satisfy his every need. But not his brother's wife, he'd assured himself disgustedly. Dear God, he'd thought, if he ever got that desperate, he'd go out and buy a gun.

Not that his attitude had deterred Fleur. On the contrary, she'd seemed to find his resistance very appealing. It became a point of honour with her to succeed, and not until he threatened to tell Chase did her provocation cease.

Of course, that was a dozen years ago now, and Matthew had long stopped worrying about his brother. His own career—first as a newspaper columnist, and then as an overseas reporter working for an agency based in New York—had broadened his mind, and he was no longer surprised by anything people did. Working in wartorn Lebanon and South-east Asia, he'd become inured to man's inhumanities to man. The problem of a sex-hungry sister-in-law seemed small indeed, when compared to the struggle between life and death.

Besides, in his absence, Fleur and Chase had appeared to reconcile any differences they might have had. They had both grown older, for one thing, and Matthew's different lifestyle had reinforced the barriers between them.

Then, five years ago, Matthew had written his first novel. A lot of it had been based on his own experiences in Beirut, and, to his amazement, it had been an immediate success. Film rights had been optioned; in paperback it sold almost five million copies. He'd become an overnight celebrity—and he'd found he didn't like it.

That was when he had had the notion of moving out of the United States. He'd always liked the islands of the Caribbean, and the casual lifestyle of Barbados suited him far better than the hectic social round of living in New York had ever done. When his second book was completed, he had it written into the contract that he was not available for subsequent publicity. He preferred his anonymity. He didn't want to become a media hack.

But, to his astonishment, like Fleur when he'd rejected her, his public found his detachment as intriguing as she had done. Avoiding talk-shows and signing sessions made no difference to his sales. His books apparently sold themselves, and curiosity about his lifestyle was rife.

All the same, it was a lot harder to reach him at Dragon Bay. The villa, which he had had erected on the ruins of an old plantation house, had excellent security features, and Lucas Cord—once his sound technician, but now his secretary-cum-assistant—made sure he wasn't bothered by any unwelcome guests. Matthew supposed he'd become something of a recluse, only visiting New York when he needed stimulation. He seldom invited women to Dragon Bay. He wasn't married, and he had no desire to be so.

Which was probably something else he could lay at Fleur's door, he reflected cynically, watching as a dusty estate car skidded into the parking area and a girl and two young children tumbled out. For all his brother's marriage had lasted until his death, he doubted Chase had really been happy. He'd lived his life constantly placating a woman who'd tried to cheat him at every turn.

'Henry—wait!'

The girl—or was she a young woman? Matthew was never quite sure of the distinction—yelled desperately after the small boy, who had darted recklessly between the parked cars. She seemed hung up with the other child, who appeared to be doubled up with pain, and Matthew could see an accident in the making if the boy gained the busy area where the taxis were waiting.

Without giving himself time to think about the pros and cons of what he was about to do, Matthew thrust open his door and vaulted out of the Range Rover. His long legs swiftly overtook the boy's, and his hand descended on the child's shoulder seconds before he reached the open road.

'Ouch.' The boy—Henry?—looked up at him indignantly. 'Let go of me! I'm going to meet my daddy.'

'Not without your mother, you're not,' returned Matthew smoothly, turning to look back towards the cars. 'Come along. I'll take you back. Did no one ever tell you it's dangerous to play in traffic?'

Henry looked up at him mutinously. 'I wasn't playing.'

'Nor are the drivers,' said Matthew drily, feeling the boy's resistance in every step they took. He was aware that his action had drawn some unwelcome attention, and he hoped that no one imagined he was enjoying himself.

The child's mother was hurrying towards them now, and Matthew regarded her with some impatience. With her waist-length braid and narrow body, she hardly looked old enough to have two children, albeit of pre-school age. But she had the casual elegance of many English holidaymakers at this time of year, women who knew nothing about caring for their own children, and he felt a surge of anger at her obvious lack of control.

'Oh, Henry!' she exclaimed when she reached them, bending down to grab the boy's hand with evident relief. 'Don't you ever—ever—go dashing off like that again. If—if——' she cast a swift glance up at Matthew '—this gentleman hadn't caught you, you could easily have been knocked down!'

'Perhaps if you'd held on to his hand sooner, he wouldn't have had the chance to run away,' observed Matthew shortly, aware that it was really no concern of his. It wasn't his place to tell her how to look after her children, and the deepening colour in her cheeks caused him as much discomfort as herself.

The trouble was, he realised, she had annoyed him. Driving into the car park like a mad thing, allowing the boy to put his life in danger. People like her shouldn't be allowed to have children, he thought unreasonably. Though why he felt so strongly about it, he really couldn't say.

'Yes,' she said stiffly now, facing him with eyes that were an indeterminate shade of grey. 'I know it was remiss of me to let Henry run off like that. But——' she cast her gaze down at the younger child, who Matthew could see was looking quite green '—Sophie was feeling sick again, and it all happened rather fast.'

It was a valid explanation, and Matthew knew it, but for some reason he couldn't let it go. Was it that her colouring reminded him rather too strongly of the woman he'd been forced to invite here? Or was it some lingering sense of resentment that he'd had to get involved at all? Whatever the solution, he knew that she disturbed him. And he resented that intensely.

'Wouldn't it have been more sensible, then, to leave the child at home?' he countered, and her eyes widened in obvious disbelief. He was getting in too deep, and he knew it. All it needed was for her husband to appear and he'd be totally out of his depth.

'Mr——?'

'There's Daddy!'

Before she could finish what she had been about to say, the little boy started pulling at her arm. A tall man in a business suit, trailed by a porter wheeling a suitcase on his barrow, had just emerged from the airport buildings, and Matthew's frustration hardened as the little girl set up a similar cry.

'Daddy, Daddy,' she called, her nausea obviously forgotten. 'Daddy, we're here!' She tugged at her mother's hand. 'Let me go. Let me go. I want to go and meet him.'

The young woman cast Matthew one further studied look, and then released both children as the man got near enough to hold out his arms towards them. 'Perhaps you'd like to tell their father what a hopeless case I am?' she invited coldly. 'I'd introduce you myself, but I didn't catch your name.'

Matthew's jaw compressed. 'Forget it,' he said shortly, turning away, but before he could put a sufficient distance between them the children's father came up, carrying both his offspring. He looked quizzically at his wife, and then turned his attention to Matthew.

'Do you two know one another?' he asked. Then, loosening his collar, 'God, it's bloody hot, isn't it? I can't wait to get this suit off.'

'Henry ran away,' said Sophie, before anyone else could say anything, and Henry made an effort to punch her behind his father's back. 'He did,' she added, when she'd regained her father's attention. 'He would have been run over if this man hadn't brought him back.'

'He *might* have been run over,' amended her mother evenly, refusing to meet Matthew's eyes, but her husband set both children down and held out his hand.

'Thanks a lot,' he said, shaking Matthew's hand vigorously. 'I know Henry can be quite a handful. I'm Andrew Sheridan, by the way. And I'll see he doesn't do it again.'

'Aitken,' said Matthew unwillingly, banking on the fact that it wasn't such an uncommon name, and obviously neither of them had recognised him from the jackets of his books. 'Um—actually, your wife wasn't to blame for what happened. Your little girl was sick, and——'

'I'm not——'

'Thanks, anyway.' Before his wife could complete her sentence, Andrew Sheridan intervened. He gave her a mischievous look, and then continued pleasantly, 'You'll have to come and have a drink with us some time. Give us a ring. We're renting a villa out at Dragon Point.'

'Really?' Matthew managed not to make any promises, and to his relief, out of the corner of his eye, he saw Lucas striding towards him with Fleur flapping at his heels. 'I've got to go,' he said, his polite tone disguising the dismay he'd felt at discovering they were holidaying a short distance from his estate. 'If you'll excuse me...' He inclined his head curtly, and walked swiftly away.

He heard the young woman exclaim, 'Why did you do that?' and then, almost immediately afterwards, a choking gasp, as if her husband had hit her. It brought Matthew's head round, in spite of himself, but there was no evidence that she'd been abused. On the contrary, she was staring after him, as if he'd done something wrong, her eyes wide with horror and all the colour drained out of her face.

It was crazy, because she meant nothing to him, but he was tempted to go back and ask her what the hell she thought she was doing. He'd got her off the hook, hadn't he? She should be thanking him. Not gazing at him, for God's sake, as if he was the devil incarnate.

With a grunt of impatience, Matthew swung his head round and continued towards his car. Forget it, he told himself fiercely. It was nothing to do with him. But he couldn't deny a sense of anger and irritation—and the unpleasant feeling that he'd been used.

'Who was that you were talking to?' Fleur asked, after the briefest of greetings had been exchanged—reluctant on his part, fervent on hers. She insinuated herself into the seat beside him, despite the fact that Lucas had held the rear door for her, and gazed at him enquiringly. 'A little young for your tastes, isn't she, darling?' she teased. 'Or have you acquired a liking for schoolgirls in my absence?'

'And if I have?' Matthew countered, her accent jarring on him after his exchange with the other woman. His eyes glittered maliciously. 'I'm only following in your footsteps, sister, dear. We both have peculiar tastes, don't we?'

'I'm not your sister,' hissed Fleur, as Lucas climbed good-humouredly into the seat behind them. She cast the other man a tight smile. 'Perhaps I can get some sense from you.'

'I don't know who they are,' declared Lucas ruefully. 'I've never seen them before. They're probably here on holiday. We get a lot of them at this time of the year.'

'On holiday?' Fleur's expression altered. 'Not friends of Matt's, then?'

Lucas met his employer's gaze in the rear-view mirror, and gave an apologetic shrug of his shoulders. 'Not to my knowledge,' he conceded wryly. He pulled a face at Matthew before adding, 'Did you have a good journey?'

Fleur relaxed, and for the first time since her arrival she allowed herself to show a trace of regret. 'It was— lonely,' she said, rummaging in her capacious handbag for a tissue, and using it to dab her eyes. 'I couldn't help remembering that the last time I came here Chase was with me. He loved to spend time with Matt, you know? It's sad that in recent years they spent so little time together.'

Lucas made a polite rejoinder, and Matthew bit down on the urge to tell Fleur that she knew why that was, better than anyone. He had the feeling he'd been wrong to invite Fleur here, however sorry he'd felt for her at the funeral. She hadn't really changed. She was just as ingenious as ever.

'How's Dad?' he asked now, refusing to be drawn in that direction, and Fleur gave a careless shrug.

'So long as he has his damn horses to care about, no one else seems to matter,' she declared bitterly, as Matthew joined the stream of vehicles leaving the airport, and he gave her a brief, scornful glance. They both knew that wasn't true. Ben Aitken had loved his eldest son dearly, and he'd been shattered when he was killed. What she really meant was that the older man had little time for her, and he didn't have to pretend any more now that Chase was dead.

'But he's well?' Matthew persisted, suddenly recognising the vehicle ahead of them. Andrew Sheridan was driving now, but there was no mistaking the young woman seated in the back. He'd have recognised that accusing profile anywhere. She was staring out of the rear window, and he was sure she was looking at him.

'He was. When I left.' Fleur pulled a pack of cigarettes out of her bag and put one between her teeth. 'I spent a couple of days in New York before coming here.' She scanned the dashboard for the automatic lighter. 'Dammit, where is it?'

Matthew didn't reply, and as if becoming aware that his attention had been distracted, Fleur followed the direction of his gaze. 'Oh, God,' she said disgustedly, 'it's the girl again, isn't it? Whatever is she staring at? Someone should teach her some manners.'

'Her husband, perhaps?' suggested Matthew, determinedly avoiding that cool grey gaze.

'Her husband?' Fleur was disbelieving. 'You're not telling me she's married?'

'With two children,' Matthew conceded tersely. Then, to Lucas, 'They're staying at Dragon Point.'

Lucas frowned. 'At the Parrish place?' he asked, and Matthew's brows drew together.

'Yeah, right,' he said thoughtfully, taking advantage of an open piece of road to pass the other vehicle. Then, with his nemesis safely behind him, he felt free to make the connection. 'I thought the place was occupied when I walked past there this morning.'

Fleur gave him a calculating look as she lit her cigarette. 'That man—the man who was driving the car—he was on the flight from New York.'

Matthew cast her a careless glance. 'So?'

'So—one wonders what she's been getting up to, while her husband's been away.' She inhaled, and then blew smoke deliberately into his face. 'Have you been—comforting her in his absence, I wonder?'

Matthew's jaw hardened. 'Wouldn't you like to know?' he countered, refusing to rise to her bait. 'What I do is my business, Fleur,' he added, meeting her angry gaze. 'And if you must smoke, do it in your own car. I can't stand the smell of stale tobacco.'

'You're a prig, do you know that?'

But Fleur stubbed out her cigarette before giving him the benefit of her scowl. Matthew didn't answer. It would have been far too easy to tell her what he thought she was. Besides, she already knew it. Which begged the question of why she was here...

CHAPTER THREE

IT WAS a good hour's drive back to the villa.

It shouldn't have taken so long. For most of the way the new highway meant that the road was extremely good. But Helen had already learned to her cost that traffic moved much less frenetically in Barbados than it did in London. Yet she was glad of the prolonged length of the journey to try to get herself under control. The shock she had had at the airport had left her palms moist, her knees shaking and her heart beating uncomfortably fast. Dear God, had she really seen her mother? Or was it all some incredible coincidence?

Of course, Andrew thought she was sulking because he had let the Aitken man think she was his wife. She still didn't know why he'd done it, but that embarrassment had been quickly superseded by other events. That man's name—Aitken—had been familiar, but she'd never dreamed that that was who he was. Until Fleur— if it was Fleur—had come sauntering out of the airport. Then the connection had been too much to ignore.

She expelled her breath with a shiver. Had it really been Fleur? Had it really been Chase Aitken? It had looked like Fleur—or, at least, like the pictures she had once unearthed in the attic at Conyers. James Gregory had seldom mentioned her, and he had certainly never encouraged Helen to ask questions. But the woman had been her mother, after all, and she hadn't been able to help her curiosity.

Yet, if the woman had been her mother, then Chase Aitken was evidently much younger than she'd imagined. Was that what had hurt her father so badly? The fact that his wife had left him for a man almost young enough to be his son?

30

'There's no point in sitting there brooding,' Andrew remarked suddenly, arousing her from her uneasy speculations, and Helen met his accusing gaze with some frustration. As if she didn't have enough to worry about, without Tricia's husband playing some stupid game of his own.

'I'm not brooding,' she replied, which was true. Her thoughts were far less pretty. If her mother was here on the island, what was she going to do about it? Did Fleur know her father was dead, for instance? And if she did, did she care?

'Yes, you are,' Andrew contradicted her flatly. 'What's the matter, Helen? Can't you take a joke?'

'Was that what it was?'

Helen refused to be treated like a fool, and Henry gave his father a doubtful look. 'Why did that man think you and Helen were married?' he piped up curiously, and Helen heard Andrew give an irritated snort.

'How should I know?' he exclaimed, proving he was not as indifferent to his wife's possible reaction as he'd been to Helen's. If the children accused him of perpetuating the mistake, Tricia wouldn't be at all pleased. Particularly as the Aitkens were exactly the kind of people she liked to mix with.

'Well, perhaps you should have corrected him,' Helen observed now, aware that if she wasn't careful she'd be the one blamed for assuming Tricia's identity, and Andrew scowled.

'How was I to know what you'd told him?' he demanded, refusing to let her off the hook. 'I didn't want to embarrass you, that's all. The man might have been a nuisance.'

Helen was always amazed at the lengths some people would go to protect their own positions, and she gazed at the back of Andrew's head now with undisguised contempt. What had she expected, after all? She was only the nursemaid. She just hoped Tricia wouldn't imagine she'd done something to warrant the misunderstanding.

'He was nice,' asserted Sophie, apparently deciding she had been quiet long enough. Happily, she was looking better now that she had something else to think about.

'How would you know?' asked Henry at once, seldom allowing his sister to get away with anything. 'He hurt my arm, and he called me a rude name. I'm going to tell Mummy that Helen didn't stop him.'

'You're not going to tell your mother anything,' cut in his father sharply, evidently deciding that it wasn't in his best interests to let Henry carry tales. 'Or I might just have to tell her that without Mr Aitken's intervention you'd have been minced meat.'

Henry hunched his shoulders. 'I wouldn't,' he muttered.

'You would,' said Sophie triumphantly. 'Anyway, I liked him. And I think Helen liked him, too.'

'Heavens, I don't even know the man,' Helen demurred, annoyed to find that the child had achieved what her father couldn't. Hot colour was pouring into her cheeks, and Andrew's expression revealed that he knew it.

'Who is he, anyway?' he asked. 'You never did tell me. What did you find out about him? You seemed to be having quite a conversation as I walked out of the airport buildings.'

'I don't know anything more than you do,' Helen declared, not altogether truthfully, glad that she was flushed now, and therefore in no danger of revealing herself again. 'I didn't even know his name until you asked him.' Which was true. 'He's probably another tourist. The island's full of them.'

'Hmm.' Andrew was thoughtful. 'He didn't look like a tourist to me. Unless he's been here since Christmas. You don't get a tan like that in a couple of weeks.'

'Does it matter?'

Helen didn't particularly want to talk about it, or think about it, for that matter. The image she had, of a tall dark man with the lean muscled body of an athlete, was not one she wanted to cherish. Chase Aitken, she thought scornfully, polo-player, playboy, and jock. Not to mention adulterer, she added bitterly. She hoped she'd never see him again.

Tricia was up and dressed when they arrived back at the villa. She had shed her trailing wrap in favour of a loose-fitting tunic, and her auburn-tinted hair had been brushed to frame her face. She looked much different from the languid female who had waved them goodbye, and she greeted her husband more warmly than she'd been known to do before.

'Sorry I couldn't meet you, darling,' she said, getting up from the cushioned lounge chair she had been occupying on the terrace. Set in the shade of a huge flame tree, it was an oasis of shadow in the late afternoon heat that still drenched the villa. Only the breeze from the ocean provided a warm draught of air to dry moist skin, but Tricia looked cool and comfortable, and totally relaxed.

'No problem,' said Andrew easily, bending to bestow a kiss on his wife's upturned lips. But his eyes sought Helen's as he offered the salutation, and she had the uneasy feeling that their relationship would never be the same again.

'Can we have some juice?' Henry cried plaintively, bored by his parents' demonstration of marital felicity, and his mother turned to look at him with some impatience.

'You can't be thirsty,' she said. 'I told Helen to get you both a drink at the airport. Heaven knows, you had enough time.' She glanced at her watch. 'I expected you back half an hour ago. The plane was obviously late.'

'She didn't get me a drink——' Henry was beginning indignantly, when his father chose to intervene.

'Actually the plane was on time,' he said, earning a raised eyebrow from his wife. 'But there was some hold-up with the luggage. And Helen had her hands full, because Sophie had been sick.'

'Oh.' Tricia looked somewhat distastefully at her daughter. 'Not again.'

'Yes, again,' went on Andrew evenly. 'We all had our problems, didn't we, Henry?' He gave his son a warning look. 'Now, run along and ask whoever it is your mother said is looking after us——'

'Maria,' supplied Sophie proudly, and her father smiled.

'Very well. You two go and ask Maria if she'd be kind enough to give you a drink.'

'Helen can do it,' protested Tricia, before Henry and Sophie could leave them. She carefully resumed her position on the lounger. 'As they're obviously tired, it would probably be a good idea to give them their supper early and put them to bed.'

'Oh, Mummy——'

'But I want to talk to Daddy——'

The two children both spoke at once, but Tricia just ignored them. 'You can have an early night, too, Helen,' she added, stretching out her hand towards her husband. 'I shan't need you any more today.' She sighed contentedly. 'Drew and I will enjoy a quiet evening together. It's ages since we had any time alone.'

'Helen's not a child, Trish.' Andrew came to her defence, even though she hadn't wanted him to. 'Put the brats to bed by all means, Helen. But then you must join us for supper.'

'Helen may not want to,' Tricia observed tersely, not at all pleased to have her plans overset. 'She might like a quiet evening, too.'

'We are on holiday, Trish,' retorted Andrew, just as Helen was about to agree with her. 'Besides, I'm sure you'll want to hear about the man we met at the airport. He said his name was Aitken, didn't he, Helen?' He turned back to his wife. 'Do we know anyone of that name?'

Tricia stared first at her husband, then at Helen. 'Aitken?' she exclaimed. 'Did you say Aitken?'

'That's what he said,' said Andrew maliciously, enjoying Helen's discomfort. 'The name is familiar, but I can't imagine why.'

'I can,' said Tricia suddenly, and for an awful moment Helen thought she had made the connection between Chase Aitken and her mother. But then, as the other woman began to speak again, she realised how unlikely that was. Her mother had left her father almost twenty years ago.

'Well, you won't know,' Tricia explained patiently. 'It's the name of the man who owns the house beyond the point. I asked Maria who our neighbours were, and she said his name was Aitken.' She clasped her hands together excitedly. 'D'you think it's the same man?'

'I'd say it was highly likely,' said Andrew, frowning. 'Though the chap didn't make any comment when I told him we were staying here. You'd think he'd have mentioned it, wouldn't you, Helen? Unless we offended him, of course.'

'Offended him?' exclaimed Tricia sharply, looking from one to the other of them with suspicious eyes. 'How could you have offended him? For heaven's sake, Helen, what did you say?'

Helen noticed the assumption that she was the one who must have said something to offend him, and she was just about to explain what had happened when Andrew broke in.

'Well, as you know, Sophie had been throwing up all over the car park, and the bloke came over to offer his assistance. We let him think that Helen was my wife, and I don't think he was impressed by our behaviour.'

'You did what?'

Tricia stared at her husband, aghast, as Helen wished the ground would open up and swallow her. But she had nothing but admiration for the way Andrew had turned the tables. Not only had he implicated her in his schemes, but he'd successfully neutralised any flack from Aitken's direction.

'It was just a game,' he said carelessly, draping his jacket over one shoulder and loosening his tie. 'For God's sake, Trish, I doubt if he believed it. Does Helen look like the mother of these two, I ask you? A fool could see she's far too young.'

'She's exactly four years younger than me,' said Tricia through her teeth, and Andrew gave a dismissive shrug in her direction.

'Like I said, far too young,' he remarked, grinning at her frustration. 'I'm going for a shower now. I assume we do have showers in this place?' He sauntered towards the French doors that opened into the villa. 'You can come and show Daddy where Mummy's room is, Henry. And then, while I'm changing, d'you think one of you could get me a beer?'

'Andrew!'

Tricia's temper was simmering, but he was totally un-daunted by her infuriated stare. 'Oh, and ask Maria if she'd get my suitcase,' he added. 'Unless someone else would like to oblige.'

Helen spent an uncomfortable evening on her own.

After giving the children their suppers and getting them ready for bed, she'd sent a message, via Maria, to say she had a headache, and would not be joining her em-ployers for the evening meal. Instead she'd made herself a salad, eating it in her room, with the doors and windows securely bolted.

Which was one of the reasons why it was so un-comfortable, although, compared to the other events of the day, the humidity in her room was of little im-portance. Dear God, what was she going to do? She was almost sure the woman she had seen was her mother. And she was staying just a short distance away. Oh, lord, how could she bear it?

The clipped exchange she had with Tricia, after Andrew had gone for his shower, hadn't helped. It had been useless trying to explain that Andrew hadn't ac-tually *said* she was his wife, that Aitken—she refused to think of him as Chase—had only assumed it. She hadn't even been given the opportunity to relate properly the events which had led up to his introduction, and if she'd hoped that by telling Tricia how he'd spoken to her— how he'd criticised her—the other woman might relent at all, she'd been wrong. Tricia wasn't interested in her feelings. She was only interested in the embarrassment their behaviour might have caused *her*.

'I think you behaved totally irresponsibly,' she had said, pacing up and down the terrace, and Helen had noticed how somehow she had shouldered all the blame. 'Have you seen the house beyond the point? Well, of course you must have. It's huge, Helen, and obviously expensive. The man must be seriously rich!'

'Why?' Helen had sighed. 'He could be renting the place, just as we are.'

'I doubt it.' Tricia had dismissed that idea. 'I'm fairly sure he lives here.' She had frowned. 'I wonder if he's married. I'd like to meet his wife.'

Helen groaned, and ran her hands over her hair now. The prospect of Tricia meeting the Aitkens socially was one she couldn't bear to endure. Although she doubted her mother would recognise her, her name was obviously going to give her identity away. What would Fleur do if she was introduced to her own daughter by a stranger? Would she acknowledge her? Would she care? Or was it all some awful nightmare she'd invented?

Helen was up even earlier the next morning. The ironic thing was that her body was beginning to adjust to the time-change, but the uneasy tenor of her thoughts wouldn't let her sleep. As soon as it was at all light, she crawled wearily out of bed. Perhaps a swim in the ocean might revive her, she thought tiredly. Right now the prospect of facing any of the Sheridans filled her with dismay.

Stripping off her nightgown, she went into the bathroom and cleaned her teeth. One of the ubiquitous flying beetles had committed suicide in the sink, and she

removed it to the lavatory with a handful of toilet paper.
Then, returning to the bedroom, she pulled a one-piece
maillot out of the drawer. Its high-cut hipline was rather
daring, but she doubted anyone would see her.

In any event it was black and, in spite of the fact that
she'd already spent several days in the sun, she looked
rather pale this morning. Pale and *un*interesting, she
mocked herself ruefully. Still, that was her role here: to
avoid being noticed.

Wrapping a towel about her hips, she unlocked the
shutters and crossed the balcony. Unlike a summer's
morning at home, it didn't really get light here until after
six o'clock. Then, like the twilight that lasted so briefly,
there was a rapid transference to day. The sun rose swiftly
in these semi-tropical islands, and the air was always
transparent and sweet.

Tussocky grass grew against the low wall where she'd
been sitting musing the previous day. A shallow flight
of steps gave way to the beach, and the sand felt quite
cool between her toes. It was coral sand, fine and slightly
gritty, and here and there a rockpool gave a fleeting
glimpse of shade. There were crabs, too, scuttling out
of her path, some of them so tiny they looked like shells.
And now and then a seabird came down to hunt for
food, screaming its objection to her intrusion.

When she reached the water's edge, she couldn't resist
turning her head to see the house Tricia had spoken of
the night before. It wasn't wholly visible, which was one
of the reasons Tricia had been so interested in it. All
they could see from this distance was a sprawling roof,
shaded by palms, and a coral wall. Evidence, if any was
needed, that their neighbour preferred his privacy.

Still, Tricia was right about one thing, Helen reflected
ruefully. It did look an enormous place. Compared to
the Aitken house, the villa they were renting looked tiny,
even if it did have four bedrooms and a parlour, and the
swimming-pool in the garden.

The water felt cold when she broached the tiny rivulets edged with foam that creamed about her feet. Of

course, she knew it was only the heat of her body that made her think it. Compared to the English Channel, it was like a Turkish bath.

It crossed her mind suddenly that this was the time she had seen the stranger walking along the shoreline from her balcony. And hard on the heels of this thought came the obvious knowledge of who it must be. She'd seen him often enough, and always walking in this direction. It had to be Chase Aitken, and he was bound to think she'd come to intercept him.

The idea of taking a swim instantly lost its appeal. She had no desire to encounter Chase Aitken again, and the realisation of how fine she was cutting it sent her hurrying back the way she had come. Unless he had better things to do—and her stomach hollowed unpleasantly at the thought—he'd be turning the point any moment. All that had saved her was an outcrop of rock, and a brain that was not quite vapid.

'We meet again, Mrs Sheridan.'

The voice—a far too familiar voice in the circumstances—almost scared the life out of her. She'd thought she was alone on the beach—she *had* been alone when she walked down to the water. But somehow, while she was ogling his house, perhaps, or before the coolness of the water had cleared her head, he'd negotiated the outcrop. He was sprawling in her path now, and she'd almost walked all over him.

'I'm—not—Mrs Sheridan,' she said, choosing the least controversial thing she could say. It was disconcerting to have him looking up at her, and she was glad she still had the towel securely round her hips.

'I know.' With a lithe movement he reversed their positions, his superior height making it necessary for Helen to tilt her head now. 'My—housekeeper—knows your maid, Maria. When I described you, she said you were the Sheridans' nanny.'

Helen felt a quiver of annoyance. 'Why should you describe me to your housekeeper?' she demanded. 'I don't think I like the idea of you—gossiping—about me to your staff.'

His dark eyes flickered. 'I don't gossip—Helen, isn't it? I was curious. You seemed far too young to have two children.'

Helen was angry. 'Did I?' She licked her lips. 'Well, that may be so, but I don't recall giving you permission to use my name, *Mr* Aitken,' she declared stiffly.

His mouth turned down. 'I don't know your surname, Miss——?' he mocked her carelessly. 'Why don't you tell me what it is, and I'll see what I can do?'

Helen swallowed, remembering suddenly that she shouldn't—couldn't—give this man her name. 'It doesn't matter,' she said, hoping to end the discussion. But when she moved to go past him, he caught her arm.

She wasn't afraid—although she supposed she should have been. After all, this was the man who had seduced her mother, and he was hardly likely to quibble over a nanny. Even without being aware of the lean body, partially concealed by the laced ties of his sweat-suit, the hand gripping her forearm was hard. There was strength in every finger digging into her skin, and his musky heat enveloped her in its warmth.

'What is it with you?' he asked, his breath cool against her cheek. 'Just because I spoke out of turn yesterday, you're determined to hold it against me? Look——' he released her, as if realising that force wasn't going to aid his cause '—I'll apologise, OK? If the kid's anything like his father, I guess you've got my sympathy.'

Helen caught her breath. 'And that's supposed to be an apology?'

'No.' Aitken shook his head. 'If anyone needs to apologise, it's Sheridan. He didn't correct me when I made an error of judgement. I guess he thought it was amusing. Making fun of the locals.'

Helen told herself she didn't care where he and her mother lived, but she found herself asking the question just the same. 'Are you a local, Mr Aitken? I wouldn't have thought this was quite your style.'

'But you don't know anything about my style,' he countered smoothly. 'And, as it happens, Barbados suits me very well.'

'I'm so glad.'

Helen was sarcastic, but she couldn't help it, and Aitken regarded her with studied eyes. 'So,' he said, 'I'm glad we've cleared up that misconception.' He glanced towards the water. 'Were you about to go for a swim?'

'I—no.' Helen made the decision quickly, even though the reason for her previous prevarication had now been removed.

'Shame,' he remarked. 'I thought I might join you. Swimming alone can be dangerous. Did no one tell you that?'

'Dangerous for whom?' enquired Helen tautly, and then, with a shiver of impatience, she shook her head. 'I have to get back,' she added crisply, aware that it would be fatally easy to be attracted to this man. And, because it had to be said, 'I'm sure your wife will be wondering where you are.'

'My wife!' Chase Aitken stared at her disbelievingly. 'I don't have a wife, dammit. What gave you that idea?'

Helen swallowed, incapable of answering him right away. He hadn't married her mother, then, she thought incredulously. They'd only been living together all these years. No wonder Fleur had greeted him so—so hungrily. She must never be sure he hadn't found someone else.

Helen felt a little sick. The realisation that Chase Aitken had treated her mother with as little respect as Fleur had treated her father should have been re-assuring, but it wasn't. Yet Fleur's problems were no concern of hers. She'd forfeited the right to have Helen care about her when she'd ignored her daughter's existence for the past eighteen years. Helen's nausea stemmed from her own unwilling reaction to the news. In spite of all that had happened, it was Chase Aitken's dark disturbing face that had haunted her dreams last night.

'I don't know,' she muttered at last, turning away and suppressing the urge to confront him with all she did know. She wrapped her arms about her waist. 'I'd have thought it was a reasonable assumption, considering the woman was all over you at the airport.' Her lips tightened. 'And now, if you'll excuse me, I've got a job to do.'

CHAPTER FOUR

MATTHEW strode back to Dragon Bay in a foul temper.

It might have been a novelty for him to be put down by a skinny blonde with more mouth than sense, but it didn't amuse him. He didn't even know why he'd bothered to speak to her. It wasn't as if he cared what she thought of him. He'd been civil, that was all, and she'd insulted him. What the hell did she know about his life?

For God's sake, he thought, letting himself into the grounds of his house through the iron gate set into the wall, there were plenty of women around who didn't take offence when he offered advice. Nothing could alter the fact that the boy had got away from her. So what if the other kid was being sick? She hadn't been about to choke, had she?

But it was that crack about Fleur that had really got to him. Bloody cheek, he fumed angrily. What did it have to do with her? It was little consolation to know that she'd been watching him. He'd known that, dammit. He'd seen the accusation in her face.

For once, the gardens surrounding his villa didn't appease him. Almost two acres of green lawns, flowering shrubs and brilliant flame trees provided a fitting setting for the sprawling Spanish-style villa that was his home. Cool, shaded rooms surrounded three sides of a paved courtyard, with a stone fountain in the centre whose rippling pool was edged with lilies.

Through a belt of palms, he could just glimpse the painted roofs of the cabanas, and beyond that the swimming-pool was a smooth slash of aquamarine, glinting in the sun. The way he felt right now, he would have liked to have plunged his sweating body into the cool water. But the thought that Fleur might choose to join him had him opting for a shower.

Dammit, he thought, crossing the patio, where hanging baskets spilling scarlet geraniums provided a startling splash of colour, he couldn't even do what he liked in his own home. Stepping beneath a shadowed balcony, woven with bougainvillaea, he entered a marbled hallway and mounted grimly to his suite of rooms. He'd always enjoyed his morning walks before, but today he felt decidedly out of tune with himself.

He ran the shower hot, then cold, soaping his limbs aggressively as he endeavoured to lighten his mood. Fleur couldn't stay here forever, he thought, deliberately turning his thoughts from the woman on the beach. She'd soon get bored without the social life she'd enjoyed as Chase's wife. Besides, although there were plenty of stores in Bridgetown to suit her needs, Fleur was an avid shopper. She'd spent a small fortune in beauty parlours alone, and she'd had a new wardrobe of clothes every season.

He wondered in passing where she was planning to live, now that Chase was no longer a factor. He doubted she'd stay on at the ranch, even if his father was willing. She'd always been more at home in the capital cities of the world. He couldn't see her vegetating at Ryan's Bend.

He was shaving when his assistant knocked at his door. At his shout, Lucas came into his bedroom, and Matthew paused in the doorway to his bathroom, his razor still in his hand.

'Problems?' he asked, and Lucas pulled a face.

'Your sister-in-law has already asked where you are, if that's what you mean,' he remarked, propping his stocky frame against a chest of drawers. 'She's having breakfast in the dining-room, would you believe? I thought you said she rarely got up before midday.'

'She doesn't—usually,' Matthew replied flatly, turning back to the mirror and expelling a weary breath. He cursed as the razor nicked his jaw. 'Damn, I guess that means she wants something, doesn't it? You may be right. This is not just a social visit.'

Lucas shrugged. 'Has it occurred to you that she may be short of money?'

'Of course it has.' Matthew rinsed his jaw with fresh water and turned back again, drying his face with a towel. 'But I don't see how. Chase always had insurance. And his horses were worth a small fortune, you know that.'

Lucas considered. 'Could he have been in debt?'

'I guess he could.' Matthew frowned. 'But if he was, he never said a word to me. And wouldn't he have discussed it with my father?' He grimaced. 'Perhaps he did. The old man always was as close-mouthed as a shrew.'

A shrew...

Matthew tossed the towel aside, annoyed to find that the connotations of that particular word were not to his liking. It reminded him again of the young woman he had encountered on the beach. The truth was, for all his irritation with her, she had disrupted his morning walk and his equilibrium. And where that disturbance was rooted, he didn't care to consider.

'So, what are you going to do?' Lucas watched as Matthew tossed the towel aside and pulled on a pair of frayed denim shorts and a loose black T-shirt. 'Ask her right out? Or let her make the first move?'

'That depends.' Matthew forced his thoughts back to Fleur, and scanned the bedroom with narrowed eyes. Then, observing that his watch was lying on the cabinet where he had left it, he went to pick it up. 'I don't intend to allow her to stay here indefinitely.'

'So you'll play it by ear,' remarked Lucas, straightening. 'D'you want to look over the manuscript this morning, or shall I concentrate on the accounts?'

Matthew gave him a resigned look. 'What do you think?'

Lucas grinned, his fair features crinkling humorously. 'Accounts it is,' he said. 'And I'll eat breakfast in the kitchen. I'm not sure I'm in the mood for Fleur's particular kind of chat.'

'And I am?' queried Matthew drily, buckling the slim gold Ebel on to his wrist. 'Remind me to thank you for your support some time, won't you? I don't know what I'd do without you in circumstances like this.'

Leaving the spacious, if slightly austere surroundings of Matthew's bedroom behind, both men walked along the wide gallery that connected all the rooms on the upper floor. Open on one side at present, with sculptured arches giving an uninterrupted view of the ocean, there were tight-fitting shutters which could be closed if a tropical storm blew in from the Gulf. In the latter months of the year there was the risk of hurricanes, too, but thankfully they were few and far between. In the main, the weather was fairly temperate, with humidity being the biggest source of complaint.

They descended the shallow staircase Matthew had climbed earlier, where a glistening chandelier hung from a central bracket. The dining-room, where Fleur was having breakfast, opened on to the inner courtyard, and Matthew left Lucas to his own devices while he trod along the cloistered veranda.

The dining-room was far too big for one person. Matthew had always thought so, although its cream and green décor always gave him pleasure. It was spacious and airy, but on lamplit evenings it could be warmly intimate as well. Like every other apartment in the villa, it was aesthetically appealing as well as functional, and those guests who had been invited here had been agreeably impressed.

Even so, Fleur looked mildly intimidated, sitting at the long oak table. Ruth, his housekeeper, had laid two places at the end of its dark polished surface, and his sister-in-law's expression was reflected in the glaze of fragile china and silver tableware. She was picking rather desultorily at the dry toast set in front of her, a cup of black coffee at her elbow indicating that she was still far too anxious about her weight.

But her features warmed considerably when Matthew appeared in the doorway. Her eyes, already carefully outlined with mascara, lit up, and she patted the chair beside her, as if there were anywhere else he was likely to sit.

'Good morning, darling,' she greeted him affectionately. 'I was beginning to wonder if I'd have to eat alone.'

'Eat?' remarked Matthew drily, indicating the dry toast on her plate. 'Didn't Ruth offer you a croissant? She makes them herself, and they're delicious.'

'They're also about five thousand calories,' exclaimed Fleur, exaggerating as usual. She shuddered theatrically. 'They're full of fat, Matt. You really shouldn't eat them. You may not realise it now, but they can shorten your life.'

'So can smoking,' replied Matthew pointedly, and Fleur dropped her handbag back on to the floor. 'So— did you sleep well?'

Fleur grimaced. 'I never sleep well,' she declared. 'Ever since Chase died, I've lain awake for hours, wishing he was there. I'm a physical person, Matt. I need someone to hold me. But there hasn't been anyone to do that for such a long, long time.'

Matthew's lips compressed. 'Chase has only been dead a couple of months.'

'I know that.' Fleur gave him a defensive stare. 'But—— Well, you might as well know, Chase and I had been having problems. It's—almost a year since we—we slept together.' She gave Matthew an appealing look. 'You don't know what it was like. He was such a jealous man!'

Matthew's stomach muscles tightened. 'What you mean is, you were screwing him around,' he stated, and she gave a protesting cry.

'No. No, I wasn't,' she exclaimed bitterly. 'I'm not that sort of woman.' And then, as Matthew gave her a scorching look, she added swiftly, 'You—you were the exception. I was lonely. And you always were such a— such an attractive boy—*man*.'

Ruth appeared at that moment, and Matthew was relieved. He doubted he could have responded to Fleur without rancour. His gut was telling him he'd been a fool to invite her here, but with his conscience eating at him there'd seemed nothing else he could do.

'You like some more coffee, Mrs Aitken?' Ruth asked, after taking Matthew's order for scrambled eggs. A Czechoslovakian immigrant, Ruth had first worked for her employer in New York, but she'd been more than happy to accompany him when he relocated to the Caribbean.

'What?' Fleur seemed distracted, and she regarded the plump housekeeper with some impatience. 'Oh—no. No. Nothing else at the moment. And be sure you cook the eggs with sunflower oil. It's better for the digestion.'

'Just do as you normally do,' Matthew put in evenly, as Ruth looked dismayed. He helped himself to some freshly squeezed orange juice and regarded his sister-in-law with some dislike. 'After almost ten years, Ruth knows how I like my eggs. And add a couple of bacon rashers,' he appended, giving the woman a smile.

Ruth departed, looking slightly reassured, and Fleur met Matthew's eyes without remorse. 'All that cholesterol,' she declared. 'You'll regret it when you're older.'

'Like you, you mean?' he suggested, in no mood to be charitable. 'Just give it a rest, will you? I don't need you to run my life.'

Fleur looked longingly at her bag, but something—a desire to placate him, perhaps, Matthew thought wryly—kept her from reaching for her cigarettes. Instead, she pushed her plate aside and folded her arms on the table, giving him an innocent smile, as if butter wouldn't melt.

'So,' she said. 'What are we going to do today?'

'We?' Matthew regarded her over the top of his glass. 'I don't know what you're going to do, but I've got a book to write.' He paused. 'You can swim, or sunbathe, or go shopping if you'd rather. There's a car at your disposal, and Bridgetown has plenty of shops for you to try.'

Fleur wrinkled her nose. 'I know what Bridgetown has,' she said shortly. 'It's not that long since I've been here.' She hesitated. 'I was hoping you might take me sightseeing. When we were here before, Chase hardly left the house.'

Remembering how tired his brother had looked the last time he saw him did not endear his widow to Matthew at this moment. 'You don't really expect me to believe you want to go sightseeing, do you?' he asked harshly. 'When was the last time you visited a museum, or a cathedral, or watched cruise ships unloading at the quay?' He set down his empty glass with careful precision. 'I may be gullible, but I'm not still wet behind the ears, Fleur. Do what you like, with pleasure, but don't include me.'

Fleur gave him a wounded look. 'You'll never forget that one mistake, will you? I let you see how frustrated I was, God knows how many years ago, and you can't accept that I've changed. I loved Chase, Matt, you've got to believe me.' She waited a beat. 'And I don't think he'd appreciate your treating me like a leper.'

Matthew forced himself to calm down. 'All right,' he said. 'If that's what you'd like, I'll have Lucas show you around. There are some flower caves in Saint Lucy that are well worth a visit, and several old plantation houses on your way.'

Fleur looked sulky. 'You're just being unpleasant,' she said. 'You know I don't want Lucas to take me anywhere. When you invited me here, I assumed it was because you wanted my company. I didn't think I was to be given the brush-off because you want to work.'

Matthew expelled a heavy breath. 'You know why I invited you here, Fleur.'

'Do I?'

'You should.' He looked at her with less than sympathetic eyes. 'You want the truth? I felt sorry for you. Good God, you practically begged me to let you come here. You said you couldn't stand being at the ranch another day.'

Fleur sniffed. 'So? What's changed?'

'Nothing's changed. That's what I'm saying.' Matthew struggled to be patient. 'You're welcome to spend a couple of weeks here. I can guess things were pretty grim for you at Ryan's Bend. As you say, my father has the horses to keep him busy. Until you decide what you're going to do—where you're going to live—it isn't going to be easy.'

Fleur heaved a sigh. 'You don't understand,' she said, running her fingernail round the rim of a spoon. 'I don't know what I'm going to do—how I'm going to manage. Chase left so little money, and I don't have any of my own.'

'Wait a minute.' Matthew felt the first glimmerings of apprehension. 'What do you mean? Chase was broke?'

'Near enough,' she conceded, her fingers curling into her palms. 'I didn't know until—until afterwards. After all those years of competing and winning prizes, I assumed——' She pressed her lips together. 'But your father put me straight on that account. Did you know he even owned all the horses Chase rode?'

Matthew frowned. 'What about the insurance?' He paused. 'I know Chase was insured. He was very particular about that sort of thing.'

Fleur shrugged her narrow shoulders. 'Well—they wouldn't pay out.'

'What?'

Matthew was appalled, and Fleur shifted rather discomfitedly in her seat. 'Don't look at me like that. It wasn't my fault,' she protested. 'He—he'd been drinking before the—before the game when—it happened.'

'Chase?'

'Yes, Chase.' Fleur tilted her head. 'That's why they wouldn't pay. They said he was to blame.'

Matthew pushed back his chair and got up from the table, unable to sit still as the import of what she was saying assaulted his senses. He'd assumed until then that Chase's death had been a terrible accident. Now Fleur was telling him that Chase had broken the rules.

'Why?' he said now, turning to face her, and Fleur gazed at him with uncomprehending eyes.

'Why, what?'

'Why had he been drinking?' snarled Matthew. 'As I recall, Chase didn't even like the stuff. Why would he swallow alcohol when he knew he had to play?'

'Don't ask me.' Fleur gave him an indignant look. 'I wasn't his keeper. Besides, perhaps you didn't know him as well as you thought you did. In recent months, he'd been drinking quite a lot.'

Matthew pushed his hands into the pockets of his shorts, aware of an overwhelming urge to shake Fleur until he got the truth. Oh, he didn't doubt there was some truth in what she was saying. But the reasons for Chase's behaviour had not been explained.

A feeling of regret assailed him. It was true that in recent months he hadn't seen as much of either Chase or his father as he should have. And the ironic thing was, it had been because of Fleur that he'd stayed away from his home. He'd always been conscious of what had happened, however much he'd tried to ignore it. And it had been easier for him to avoid the ranch, and the unpleasant memories it evoked.

'I think——' Fleur started, and even though Matthew gave her a warning look, she pressed on anyway. 'I think he knew his game was failing,' she declared firmly. 'His average was falling, and I know he was worried about staying in the team. You know what polo-players are like: they have this macho image. I think Chase was afraid he was losing it. He was the oldest man on the field.'

Matthew's eyes narrowed. 'How would you know?'

Fleur held his gaze for a defensive moment, and then looked down at her plate. 'I hope you're not implying what I think you're implying,' she said, her voice constricted. 'I told you: I loved your brother, Matt. Whatever you think, I miss him every day.'

Matthew turned away, staring bleakly towards the glistening ocean. He missed Chase, too. More than he could ever have imagined. Dammit, that was why he'd invited Fleur here. To try and assuage the guilt that he still felt.

'If you want me to leave, I will,' Fleur offered in an unsteady voice, and Matthew squashed the uncharitable thought that her words were calculated. But there was no denying her ability to take advantage of a situation, and she must be pretty sure he wouldn't take her up on it, or she'd never have taken the risk.

'Forget it,' he said now, but when Ruth brought his breakfast it was an effort to attack the food. He felt sick even thinking about what Chase might have suffered during the last months of his life. If he had been worrying about his future, why the hell couldn't he have said?

An hour later he was sitting at his desk, wondering if he should call his father, when Lucas buzzed his private line. Lucas monitored all incoming calls from his office, and Matthew seldom took unsolicited calls, unless they were from people he knew.

'You've got a call,' Lucas announced ruefully. 'From Andrew Sheridan. I can tell him that you're out, if you like—or busy. But I thought I'd better clear it with you first.'

Matthew frowned. To say he knew Andrew Sheridan was certainly an exaggeration. And, as Lucas knew nothing about his encounter with Helen on the beach, he knew he thought it was just a formality. But, in spite of himself, Matthew was intrigued. And there were other considerations here that made him say, quite uncharacteristically, 'I'll speak to him.'

'You will?'

Lucas couldn't hide his surprise, and Matthew guessed his assistant thought he was being rather foolish. But, 'Why not?' he said, wondering what else the day could throw at him. 'We can't live like hermits while Fleur's here.'

'If you say so.'

Lucas sounded off-hand, but he connected the call at once and rang off. It was just curiosity, Matthew told himself, determining to be civil. He was curious about Andrew Sheridan's relationship with Helen. It had occurred to him that it might not be as innocent as it seemed.

'Aitken?'

Andrew Sheridan's voice was one of those upper middle class English voices, and it grated on Matthew's nerves this morning. It seemed to imply that he should be glad to hear from him, that as a commonplace colonial he was being honoured.

'Sheridan,' he offered in response, wishing he'd taken Lucas's advice after all and avoided the call. It wasn't as if he was finding it easy to concentrate in any case, and the idea that Helen might be having an affair with her employer was already assuming far too much importance.

'I hope you don't mind me ringing, old man,' Andrew exclaimed jovially. 'My lady wife insisted that I call and put the record straight. The young lady you saw me with yesterday wasn't Mrs Sheridan. She's our nanny, actually. It was all a rather bad joke.'

Matthew didn't make the mistake of admitting his knowledge this time. 'No problem,' he said, unwillingly relieved that Helen apparently hadn't mentioned their encounter on the beach. And then, untruthfully, 'I never gave it another thought. Whoever she was, she seemed to have her hands full.'

'Well, yes.' Andrew sighed. 'I'm afraid Henry and Sophie *are* something of a handful for her. Poor Helen hasn't had a lot of experience. We may have to let her go if something like that happens again.'

Matthew felt unreasonably resentful on her behalf. 'I doubt if anyone could have coped any better,' he declared coolly. 'Perhaps if she hadn't had to bring the children to the airport in the first place, there wouldn't have been a problem.' He paused. 'Is your wife an invalid, Sheridan? I'm just wondering why they didn't stay with her, when the little girl obviously suffers from car sickness.'

Andrew Sheridan was unnaturally silent for a moment, and Matthew hoped that he was offended. He had no desire to get involved with any of the Sheridans, and, despite his instinctive defence of her, the less he saw of their nanny the better.

'So, in your opinion, it was just a chapter of accidents,' Andrew said at last, and Matthew acknowledged that he'd underestimated Sheridan's persistence. 'I'm glad about that. Helen's an engaging creature, isn't she? I wouldn't like to dismiss her, when she's had such a lot of bad luck.'

The desire to ask what bad luck he was talking about was pressing, but Matthew contained himself with difficulty. It had been said for just that reason, to inspire his curiosity, and after this morning's little fiasco he was not about to bite.

'Anyway,' Andrew went on, when it became obvious that Matthew wasn't going to fall for that line, 'I didn't ring to discuss the merits—or otherwise—of the children's nursemaid. No, I'm ringing to ask you and your—well, partner—to have drinks with us tomorrow evening. What do you say?'

'Oh, I——' Matthew was on the point of refusing when the image of an indignant woman, with misty grey eyes and sun-streaked hair, swam before his eyes. In spite of the anger she had aroused in him, he was not averse to giving her a taste of her own medicine. After all, she'd accused him of neglecting his wife, just because she'd seen him with Fleur at the airport. It might be amusing to take Fleur with him, just to see how she responded to that.

'I know you must be a busy man,' Andrew added, obviously aware of Matthew's ambivalence, 'but we would appreciate the chance to make amends. And I know Trish would love to meet you. She's admired your house so often on her walks along the beach.'

Matthew hesitated. 'Well——'

But his mind was already made up. It would amuse Fleur, he knew, and get her off his back for a couple of hours. Besides which, he was in a mood for action. His doubts about Chase's death had only fuelled his sense of guilt...

CHAPTER FIVE

HELEN stood in her bedroom, trying to calm her nerves. Ever since Andrew had told her that Chase Aitken and his 'partner' were coming for drinks this evening, she had been in a state bordering on panic, and it wasn't getting any better.

It was all very well telling herself that her mother hadn't recognised her, and therefore she had no reason for her anxiety— but it didn't work. What if either Tricia or Andrew used her surname? Combined with her age and appearance, wasn't the coincidence just too great?

She felt sick, too, but that was mostly hunger. She'd hardly eaten a thing since lunchtime the previous day. As soon as Andrew had dropped his bombshell her throat had closed up and her appetite had vanished. She was afraid of what might happen, and nothing could alter that.

Yet she had nothing to be ashamed of. She hadn't abandoned her husband and small daughter and taken off with a man who was far too young for her. Oh, she knew there were no hard and fast rules about relationships. She'd even heard of cases where an older woman and a younger man were very happy together. But not at the expense of their families; not when they had children to leave behind . . .

Damn her, she thought painfully. Damn Fleur, and damn Chase Aitken. Why had it had to be him who came to her assistance at the airport? Why couldn't it have been some stranger, instead of her mother's playboy lover?

Of course, she might be able to avoid them. Tricia hadn't invited her to join them, but that might be because she expected her to do so anyway. In London things

had been different. Then Helen had only joined her employer for supper if Andrew Sheridan had been out of
town. But since arriving in Barbados there'd been no
lines of demarcation, and although the first night
Andrew arrived she'd managed to evade their company,
last night she hadn't been so lucky.

Privately, she suspected they found an undiluted diet
of one another's company boring. They seldom dined
alone at home, and when they went out it was always
with friends. Tricia said they were sociable animals, but
Helen suspected that without diversion their marriage
might not survive.

Which didn't help her, she thought now, slapping away
one of the annoying sandflies that had found its way
into her bedroom. Could she pretend to have another
headache? She didn't think Andrew would believe her.
But surely Tricia wouldn't care, when she was getting
her own way about Chase Aitken.

'Helen . . .'

A sleepy voice from the doorway alerted her to the
fact that Sophie, at least, had not settled down after her
day in the sun. The little girl's face was flushed, and
Helen guessed she had been taking her hat off again.
Neither child liked wearing headgear, but the heat made
protection essential.

'What is it?' Helen asked now, thinking how adorable
the little girl looked in her frilly baby-doll pyjamas.
'You're supposed to be fast asleep.'

'I'm thirsty,' said Sophie, pleading the perennial excuse
of children everywhere. 'And Henry's got Matilda, and
he won't give her back.'

'Oh, dear.' Abandoning any thought of dressing for
the evening, Helen pulled a baggy T-shirt over her shorts
and accompanied the little girl back to the children's
bedroom.

Henry was pretending to be asleep, clutching the rag
doll that Sophie had had since she was a baby. Matilda,
as she called her, was very old now, and a little tatty,
but she went everywhere with her, and especially to bed.

Walking into the adjoining bathroom, Helen got Sophie a glass of water and then approached Henry's bed. The little boy's eyelids were tightly closed, but their twitching gave him away. However, it suited her purposes to pretend she believed him, and, whisking Matilda out of his grasp, she handed her to Sophie.

Henry's eyes opened at once, but Helen was already tucking his sister into bed. 'I thought you were asleep,' she said innocently. 'And you'd forgotten to give back Sophie's doll. But if you'd like a doll of your own, I'll tell your mother. I'm sure we could find you one in town.'

Henry's jaw jutted. 'I don't want a doll,' he said sulkily. 'I'm not a baby, like her.'

'No, you're not,' said Helen. 'So don't behave like one. Now, I don't want any more nonsense tonight.'

Henry pursed his lips, but then evidently decided it wasn't worth his while to make threats. Instead, he looked at Helen slyly. 'Is that what you're wearing for supper?' he asked. 'That man and woman are already here. Did you know?'

Helen's stomach hollowed. She hadn't known. But then, that wasn't so surprising. Her room faced away from the terrace, where the Sheridans were no doubt entertaining their guests.

'Oh—I expect I'll have supper in my room,' she declared offhandedly, assuming an indifference she was far from feeling. 'Now—you two settle down. If you're quiet, and still awake when I come back, I may just read you a story.'

'Honestly?'

Henry sounded pleased, but she could see he was having difficulty in keeping his eyes open. As for Sophie, she was already on the edge of sleep, and Helen felt a reassuring sense of pride in her achievement. After all, four months ago she hadn't known the difference between pre-schoolers and toddlers. Now, she could prepare nursery meals, mop up every kind of mishap and handle childish tantrums without hesitation. To all intents and purposes, she was their guardian, and while she might still have reservations she liked her work.

She was closing the children's bedroom door when she turned to find Andrew behind her. For an awful moment, she thought it was Chase Aitken, and her face turned quite pale in the lamplight.

'Are you all right?'

Whatever Andrew had been going to say, he'd noticed her sudden pallor, and she scrubbed her hands across her cheeks to produce some spurious colour. 'You—you startled me, that's all,' she said quickly. 'I was just getting Sophie a drink.'

'And then you're going to join us, right?' he essayed smoothly. His eyes twinkled. 'Though not in shorts and a T-shirt. I don't think Trish would approve.'

Helen caught her lower lip between her teeth. 'I don't think your guests are interested in meeting me,' she said carefully. Her hand went instinctively to her hair. 'I'm sure they'll be gone before I can put on a dress.'

'Don't you believe it.' Andrew was in annoyingly high spirits. 'I've invited them for supper. Now, hurry up and get ready.'

Helen felt indignant. Apart from anything else, now that Henry and Sophie were settled for the night, the Sheridans really had no right to order her movements. Besides, the idea of going out there and facing her mother was not something she wanted to anticipate.

'I'm tired,' she said, aware that although she'd washed her hair that morning her braid was less than tidy now. Strands of honey-blonde silk were nudging her ear-lobes, and there was a definite fringe of moistness at her nape.

'We're all tired, Helen,' said Andrew, his tone a little less conciliatory now. 'Don't be difficult. Aitken has already asked where you are this evening. I don't want everyone thinking that we treat you like some latter-day Cinderella.'

Helen sighed. 'They won't do that.'

'No, they won't. Because you're going to wash your face and hands and come and meet our guests. For heaven's sake, Helen, I thought you'd be amused. It's not as if you lead an active social life. Make the most of it while you can.'

Helen's jaw trembled. 'And if I don't?'

Andrew's expression hardened. 'Well, no one can force you,' he drawled. 'I'll tell Trish you're tired, shall I? I'm sure she'll be sympathetic.'

Helen was equally sure that she wouldn't. And Andrew knew that, damn him. That was why he'd said it. The next step was to ask her if she thought she really had the stamina to do the job she was employed to do. And, although she was sure it wouldn't be easy for them to find her replacement here, she couldn't take that chance.

'I'll be ready in fifteen minutes,' she mumbled, brushing past him to reach the door of her room, but he was determined to have his pound of flesh.

'What did you say?' he asked, though she was sure he'd heard her. And when she repeated it, her face flushed and mutinous, he smiled. 'Oh, good. I knew you'd change your mind. But make it ten minutes, will you? You don't want to miss all the fun.'

Helen closed her door in his triumphant face, wishing she wasn't such a coward. But, whatever happened, she still had a living to earn. However afraid—*apprehensive*—of facing her mother she might be, she couldn't afford to lose her job over it.

All the same, she viewed the contents of her wardrobe with some misgivings. What did you wear to meet the mother you hadn't seen for eighteen years? She had no desire for Fleur to think she was competing with her. But, the fact remained, her pride wouldn't let her dress without restraint.

She finally settled on a long-waisted, button-through voile with a flared hem. The dress almost reached her ankles, but the buttons ended at her knees, leaving a provocative opening that made walking that much easier. The pattern of tiny blue and green flowers on a cream ground was attractive, and with a V-neck and elbow-length sleeves, it was neither too casual nor too formal.

She brushed her hair and plaited it again for coolness, scraping it back from her face with a determined hand. The style made her look plain, she thought, unaware that her delicate features could never be deemed severe. Instead, the fine veins at her temple were exposed, and the sensitive curve of her neck.

A flick of mascara and an application of a plum-coloured lip-gloss completed her preparations, and she stepped back from her mirror with a quickening heart. She was as ready as she'd ever be, she thought, wetting her lips deliberately. She didn't think she resembled her mother, but time would tell.

She wasn't wearing any tights, and, stepping into high-heeled sandals, she gave her room a wistful look. What she wouldn't give to be spending the evening incommunicado. Tricia should have warned her that she wanted a slave, not an employee.

She heard voices as she approached the terrace—well, Andrew's and Tricia's voices, anyway, she conceded, wondering what Chase Aitken really thought of his hosts for the evening. She'd been absolutely amazed when Tricia had told her he'd accepted their invitation. She'd had the feeling at the airport that he resented people like them.

It was a beautiful evening. Barbados was lucky in that it had few annoying insects, and it was perfectly acceptable to serve a meal outside, even after dark. With that in mind, Tricia had had Maria set a table on the terrace, and flickering Spanish lanterns added intimacy to the scene.

To avoid looking at the group of people gathered around the drinks trolley, Helen paid particular attention to the table. A centrepiece of ivory orchids and scarlet hibiscus looked wonderful against white linen, the dark green leaves contrasting richly with the carefully chosen blooms.

Tall crystal glasses gave back a multitude of colours in the candlelight, and neatly folded napkins were set at every place. *Six* places, Helen was noticing curiously, when Andrew looked round and saw her.

'At last,' he said, and for all his suave smile Helen knew he wasn't suited. 'Our dear nanny has chosen to join us. Perhaps now we can have some food.'

'Drew,' reproved Tricia, with an apologetic smile for their guests. 'Ask Helen what she'd like to drink.' But she looked the younger woman over rather critically, and Helen had the feeling she wasn't pleased either.

'Hello, again.'

Chase Aitken's low, attractive drawl forced Helen to acknowledge the other people present. But she didn't look at him, or at the third female in the group. Instead, she allowed her gaze to alight on someone she didn't know. A stocky, fair man with glasses, who was none the less familiar.

'What would you like, Helen?' Andrew was asking, and glad of a moment's grace she pretended to give the matter some thought.

'Oh—um, a glass of white wine, please,' she said, aware that both Chase and Fleur were watching her. Her mouth dried in nervous anticipation as Tricia came with evident reluctance to perform the introductions.

'Oh, yes,' she said, and Helen was obliged to meet Chase's dark appraising eyes. 'Of course, you've met, haven't you? But, Fleur—this is our saviour. Helen— this is Mrs Aitken.'

He'd lied!

That was the first thing that came into Helen's mind as she turned to the colourfully-dressed female at his side. Chase was all in black—an appropriate choice for him, she thought—but, in a floral chiffon gown and incredibly high heels, Fleur looked like a bird of paradise beside a hawk. Her hair, which had once been a similar colour to Helen's, was tinted a pale silvery shade, and tied back with a scarf that matched her outfit. The ends were loose and flowing, and trailed seductively across her bare shoulder.

Helen swallowed. When she'd seen her mother at the airport it had been from a distance. She hadn't been able to see the ravages time had wrought. But it was obvious that Fleur had had at least one face-lift, and her skin had lost the dewy freshness of youth.

Even so, her mother looked totally at ease in these surroundings. As well she might, thought Helen bitterly, if the house she had glimpsed from the beach was anything to go on. The Sheridans' villa was modest in comparison. Andrew might be well off, but he couldn't compete in Chase Aitken's league.

But such considerations were just a way of avoiding the inevitable. She couldn't believe she was standing just an arm's length from the woman who had borne her. The fact that Tricia hadn't used her surname wasn't important. Couldn't Fleur see she was her daughter? Surely she must?

Evidently not.

'How do you do?'

Fleur was holding out a languid hand, and Helen had, perforce, to take it. But she drew her hand away again with some aversion—an aversion she hoped wasn't evident to anyone else but her.

'I must say, I think you're awfully lucky to be working in such lovely surroundings,' Fleur continued, apparently noticing nothing amiss. 'Believe me, not all employers are so generous. And working with children must be rather nice.'

How would you know?

Helen wanted to say the words out loud, but commonsense—*cowardice*—kept her silent. Besides, did she really want to have anything to do with the woman? Revealing her identity to her could only hurt herself.

'And I'm Lucas,' said the man Helen had thought she recognised, evidently getting impatient with the delay. He drew her attention away from the others and shook her hand warmly. 'I'm Matt's personal dogsbody, for want of a better word.'

Helen frowned. *Matt*? But Lucas was speaking again, and she had no time to give it any attention. 'I saw you at the airport, too.' His eyes twinkled behind his glasses. 'Just from a distance, I'm afraid.'

Of course. Helen managed a smile. That was where she'd seen him. He must have gone to meet Fleur from the plane while her husband waited with the Range Rover.

'There you are. One white wine, as requested.'

Andrew had returned with her drink, and his intervention enabled Chase to ease himself between her and his assistant. 'Something wrong?' he asked in an undertone, arms folded across the black silk at his midriff. 'I take it you don't like my house-guest either. Or are you simply averse to her because she's related to me?'

Helen pressed her lips together, aware that he had successfully isolated her on the edge of the group. 'You admit it, then,' she responded huskily. 'She is related to you!'

'Sure.' He frowned. 'But she's not my wife, as you assumed the other day. She's my sister-in-law, actually. She was married to my brother. But he was killed in a riding accident two months ago.'

Helen's jaw dropped. 'He's dead!' she breathed in a staggered voice. 'I didn't know.'

'Why should you?' He was regarding her dispassionately. 'It's not as if it would make the newscasts in England. Chase was a polo-player. Not a football star.'

'Chase...' Helen said the name again, almost wonderingly, and Matthew Aitken looked at her with curious eyes.

'You didn't know him, did you?' he asked. 'That's not why you were so agitated yesterday? I know we look—*looked*—a little alike, but he was eight years older than me.'

'No.' Helen couldn't let him think that. Who knew what he might say to her mother if he suspected there was some connection? 'I—I was just sorry to hear he was dead, that's all. I expect you miss him badly. I'm sorry if I was rude.'

'When?' Matthew's lips twitched. 'At the airport? On the beach? Just now?'

'At all,' said Helen firmly, realising he was getting far too friendly. 'Um—do you live on the island, Mr Aitken? Or is this just a holiday for you, too?'

'Matthew,' he said softly. 'My name's Matthew, but most people call me Matt. And, yes, I do live here, as it happens. I find the climate and the people suit my mood.'

'Could you go and tell Maria we're ready to eat, Helen?'

Tricia had just noticed the younger woman was monopolising their most interesting guest, and her eyes flashed warningly in Helen's direction. It occurred to Helen suddenly that she had only been invited to the party because Matthew Aitken had brought his assistant. Tricia hated uneven numbers, even if it did mean she'd been forced to ask the nanny to join them.

'Of course,' she said now, glad to put some distance between herself and her mother. For all she hadn't said anything, Helen had been conscious of Fleur's proximity, and of the fact that she looked at Matthew with hot, possessive eyes. Dear God, was she already looking for Chase's replacement? And, if she was, did Matthew share his brother's fascination for diminutive blondes?

The idea was distasteful, and as she hurried into the villa Helen had to admit that it wasn't just because Fleur was her mother. The thought of Matthew Aitken making love to his dead brother's wife was repulsive. In fact, the thought of her mother even considering it caused a violent sense of injustice to invade her heart. If only her father had known he was well rid of her. Instead of spending the rest of his life trying to prove himself a man.

CHAPTER SIX

'YOU'RE so lucky living here,' Tricia Sheridan remarked enviously as they sat at the dinner table later. 'Tell me—Matt.' She gave a coy little smile to cover her audacity, and then continued, 'What do you do with yourself all day?'

Matthew couldn't make up his mind about that. But, after all, his pen-name was *Mallory* Aitken. It was possible she'd never seen his picture on the back of one of his books. He'd just got so accustomed to people using his writing as a lever that he'd become rather cynical.

'Oh—this and that,' he volunteered now, his eyes drifting irresistibly across the candlelit table. They'd seated Lucas beside Helen, and he seemed to be enjoying himself. And Helen didn't look as anxious as she'd done when she first appeared.

He wondered what Lucas was saying to her, and then chided himself for even caring. It wasn't as if he intended to see any of them again. His initial reluctance to get involved with these people had probably been right. For all Helen had offered some kind of an apology, he still had the feeling he should quit while he was ahead.

'What kind of this and that?' Tricia persisted, and Matthew wondered if it was possible to escape these proceedings without telling the truth. The last thing he needed was spurious congratulation, but before he could make a comment Fleur intervened.

'Haven't you heard of Mallory Aitken?' she exclaimed, and Matthew knew it was a measure of her annoyance at being ignored that had caused her to speak so caustically. Besides which, she had always denigrated his success before, declaring that his novels were little more than fantasy. But, 'Good heavens,' she added now,

'I thought everyone had read at least one of Matt's thrillers. They sell in their millions. Isn't that right, darling?'

Matthew managed to disguise his frustration, and gave a careless shrug of his shoulders. 'They sell,' he agreed mildly, realising it had been a bigger mistake than he'd thought bringing Fleur here. And, dammit, if he hadn't been so bloody curious about the nursemaid, he'd have had the sense to see it.

'Don't be modest, darling,' Fleur protested, her shrill laugh drawing the attention of everyone at the table. 'I'm sure Lucas has been telling Ellen how lucky he was to land this assignment. He was just Matt's sound technician, you know, when Matt worked for the ITC.'

Ellen? Matthew's mouth drew down, and glancing at the young woman in question he glimpsed a look of anguish on her face. But why? What had Fleur said to upset her? Surely getting her name wrong wasn't a reason for such distress?

'I say, how exciting!' Andrew Sheridan joined the discussion before his wife could voice her reaction. 'Mallory Aitken, eh?' His eyebrows arched. 'What did you say you'd written, old man?'

'I didn't,' said Matthew, hearing the tightness in his voice and controlling his temper with difficulty. 'I'm afraid my sister-in-law exaggerates. D'you mind if we change the subject?'

'Oh, but you must tell me what you're working on at the moment,' Tricia enthused eagerly, apparently deciding that he didn't mean her, and Matthew sighed.

'I never discuss my work,' he told her flatly, lifting his wine-glass and surveying her over the rim. 'Tell me, Mrs Sheridan, when did you say you were leaving?'

'Leaving?'

For a moment she looked totally nonplussed, and Matthew felt an uncharacteristic surge of satisfaction at the thought. It wasn't his nature to be deliberately malicious—except with Fleur, he qualified bleakly—but he didn't like these people, and he didn't care if it showed.

'I thought Lucas said Tricia and Andrew had just got here.' Once again Fleur took the initiative, and in avoiding her gaze Matthew looked straight across the table into Helen's pale face. Her expression was guarded, he thought, though vaguely apprehensive, and he wondered what she was thinking as he forced her to meet his eyes.

'Did he?'

Matthew said the words carelessly, responding to his sister-in-law without deviating from his course. It irked him when Helen looked away, and he was in no mood to be polite.

'I expect I forgot,' he remarked now, putting his wineglass down on the table. 'Time goes so quickly when you're enjoying yourself.'

It wasn't a compliment, and no one could have mistaken it for one, but Maria's reappearance to collect the empty plates provided a welcome diversion. What had he eaten? Matthew wondered as the plates were taken away. Asparagus, he thought, and then chicken. What was the matter with him tonight? He didn't normally feel so aggressive—even with Fleur.

'Anyway, we're here for a month,' Tricia declared at last, evidently deciding not to take offence. 'I suppose you know Laurie Parrish, don't you? The man who owns this villa. He's a colleague of my husband's at the Foreign Office.'

'I've met him,' said Matthew evenly, wondering if he was supposed to be impressed. 'But we don't do a lot of socialising in the usual way. Lucas and I—we live a fairly hermit-like existence.'

'Really?'

Tricia exchanged a glance with her husband, and Matthew could almost feel what she was thinking about that. Well, let her, he thought wearily. He had nothing to lose. And it might keep the Sheridans off his back.

'Oh, I'm sure now that I'm here we can change all that,' Fleur put in insistently, determinedly undermining his intent. 'You must excuse my brother-in-law, Tricia.

I can tell you from experience, his bark's much worse than his bite.'

Matthew's jaw compressed, but he didn't attempt an answer. Instead, meeting his assistant's eyes, he allowed a silent acknowledgement of Lucas's caution. But it was no stretch of his abilities to shift his eyes to Helen, and although he scorned his motives he couldn't help himself.

With the meal over, the Sheridans invited their guests to take coffee seated in the lounge chairs that had been circled on the opposite side of the patio. It gave Matthew an opportunity to escape Fleur's cloying presence, and, not risking another altercation, he removed himself from danger by sitting on the steps of the veranda. He knew Fleur wouldn't join him there, being far too afraid of ants and other crawling insects, and, eschewing anything but a brandy, he stared broodingly towards the starlit horizon.

'Is anything wrong?'

Lucas's enquiry disturbed his reverie, and looking up he found his assistant and the young woman who was causing him so much self-analysis standing looking down at him. He had the distinct impression that she wasn't there through choice, but Lucas was evidently immune to her feelings. Besides, why should he suspect that there was anything more than a casual encounter between them? Hell, there *was* nothing more than a casual encounter between them, Matthew told himself savagely. It infuriated him that he should even have thought it was anything else.

'What could be wrong?' he queried now, gripping the post and hoisting himself to his feet. His smile was thin. 'I'm having an absolutely—*spiffing*—time.'

'Matt!'

Aware of Helen beside him, Lucas was justifiably embarrassed, and Matthew allowed his narrowed gaze to encompass her taut features. 'Are you enjoying yourself, Miss——? Oh, I'm sorry, but you never did tell me your name.'

'It's—Gr—Graham,' she stammered hurriedly, and then glanced behind her, as if she half expected someone to come and contradict her. 'And—yes. Your—er—that is, Lucas—he's been telling me about some of the dangerous places where he's worked.'

'Really?' Matthew's mocking eyes turned back to his assistant. 'None more dangerous than here, eh, Luke?'

'What is it with you, Matt?' Lucas was looking angry now, and, realising he was in danger of alienating the one person in this group who cared anything about him, Matthew lifted his shoulders in a placating gesture.

'I guess my liver is just objecting to the abnormally— rich diet,' he commented ambiguously, and had the doubtful privilege of noting their individual reactions. Helen just looked confused, but Lucas had caught the innuendo.

'You were the one who said we couldn't neglect Fleur while she was here,' he reminded him drily, and Matthew gave a rueful grin.

'Yeah, I did, didn't I?' he conceded, noticing almost in passing that Helen's face had grown taut. What had he said? he wondered. Was it his imagination, or had it been the mention of Fleur that had caused her to freeze up suddenly? She couldn't be jealous, could she? There was only one way to find out. 'I'm afraid my sister-in-law can be a little irritating at times, Miss—er—Graham,' he added. 'Let me apologise on her behalf.'

Helen swallowed. He could see the sudden contraction of her throat, and, although it had not been his intention to remind himself of his own unwilling re-action to her, he couldn't help watching that slender column, or prevent his gaze from moving to the slight trace of cleavage revealed by the neckline of her dress.

She had small breasts, he observed obliquely. Small, but perfectly formed. Their *retroussé* peaks pushed rather too obviously against the cloth, and he felt himself hardening totally against his will.

God, he thought incredulously, was he so desperate for a woman that even the sight of an engorged nipple could push him over the brink? She was cold, perhaps, or apprehensive—though only the lord knew why. Certainly she'd given him no reason for behaving like a callow youth. For all her controlled indifference, he still sensed that she didn't like him at all.

In consequence, when she asked coldly, 'What are you talking about?' he knew an overwhelming urge to run a protective hand over his zip. He had no desire for her to know that she had disturbed him, whatever her real feelings might be.

It took an effort, but his response sounded reasonably cool, to his ears at least. 'Fleur called you Ellen,' he reminded her pleasantly. 'I'm afraid my sister-in-law only listens to what she wants to hear. It's a little foible of hers. You must forgive her. Since my brother died, I've noticed it more and more.'

There was an irony there, but obviously Helen didn't detect it. 'I'll never——' she began vehemently, and then, as if some inner restraint had kicked into gear, she faltered. 'That is—I mean——' She looked at both men with sudden apprehension. 'I—never noticed,' she amended herself hurriedly. 'If—if you'll excuse me, I've got to go and check on the children.'

She walked swiftly away, the skirt of her long dress flapping about her ankles. Matthew also observed the involuntary sway of her hips, and the unknowingly sensuous curve of buttock and thigh. Something he was not alone in approving, he sensed impatiently, finding Lucas's attention almost as objectionable as Fleur's at that moment.

'She doesn't like you, does she?' his assistant remarked drily, after Helen had disappeared through the French windows. 'I wish I hadn't felt sorry for you now. She and I were getting along rather well.'

'Were you?'

It was a distinct effort for Matthew to be civil, and Lucas, misunderstanding the reason for his employer's attitude, pulled a rueful face. 'Yes, we were,' he said earnestly. 'And, you must admit, you didn't look very happy. I guess Fleur has been getting to you, huh?'

Matthew scowled. 'I can handle Fleur,' he declared, finishing the brandy in his glass and regarding its base dourly. 'And I don't need you to feel sorry for me either. I can get along without your girlfriend's approval, believe it or not.'

Lucas made a careless movement of his shoulders. 'She's not my girlfriend, Matt, and you know it.' He pressed his lips together. 'Not yet, anyway.' He shrugged. 'I don't suppose there's much point in getting involved with her; they're only here for a month. But I do find her damn attractive. Did you know, she's only been the Sheridans' nanny for the last three months?'

'Really?'

Matthew managed to sound totally uninterested, but Lucas evidently didn't notice. 'Yes. Apparently, her father died six or seven months ago, leaving her virtually penniless. Whatever you think of Mrs Sheridan, at least she offered Helen a job.'

'How kind.'

Matthew's tone was sardonic, but inwardly he couldn't help wondering how a girl of her background should have wound up playing nursemaid for the Sheridans. Hadn't her father had any insurance? If he'd had a daughter like Helen, he'd have made damn sure she wouldn't be penniless when he died. He frowned. What the hell, it wasn't anything to do with him. When this unholy gathering was over, he'd make sure he never saw any of them again...

'Matt...'

Fleur's petulant voice sounded in his ear, and he turned to find her coming towards them. He hoped she was bored, that she was going to ask if they could leave, but her first words were the opposite of what he wanted to hear.

'Matt, darling, Drew—Andrew, that is—has suggested we have a rubber of bridge. It's years since I've played, but you never forget the rules. Come and be my partner. I'm sure Lucas and Ellen won't mind.'

'Her name's Helen,' said Matthew grimly, before he could prevent himself, but Fleur wasn't interested in anyone's identity but her own.

'Ellen, Helen—what does it matter?' she exclaimed impatiently. 'She seems hopelessly out of her depth, from the little I could see.'

'That's not true,' said Lucas fiercely, but Matthew found he didn't want the younger man getting involved in this discussion.

'Whatever,' he said, 'it's impolite not to remember someone's name. If you start making those kinds of mistakes, Fleur, people will think you're getting old.'

Fleur's lips tightened. 'You can be a real pain sometimes, Matt, do you know that?'

'I'm also not interested in playing cards,' he averred. 'Find yourself another partner, Fleur. I'm thinking of making my escape.'

Fleur gasped. 'But you can't.'

'Why can't I?'

'Because—well, because, to use your word, it would be impolite.' Fleur turned to Lucas. 'You know I'm right, don't you?'

Lucas hesitated. 'Well——'

'Then why don't you take my place?' suggested Matthew mockingly. 'I'm sure you'd be much better at it than me. I'll just help myself to another brandy.'

'Matt!'

'Oh, Matt!'

It was difficult to decide which of them sounded the most put out, Matthew thought wryly, sauntering away. But, hell, he'd done his good deed for the day by bringing Fleur here. He wasn't in the mood to jump through hoops, whoever was pulling the strings.

In the event, it was a fairly bloodless victory. Lucas was too polite to turn Fleur down, and the Sheridans were the kind of people who didn't question the motives of their guests. Besides, listening to Fleur explain that

Matthew wasn't feeling up to it was interesting. It made him wonder what other lies she'd told without turning a hair.

He supposed he did feel a little guilty about Lucas, but he wouldn't admit that Luke had annoyed him, too. Dammit, what did he care if the other man made it with the nursemaid? Fleur was probably right; Helen acted as if she was only here on sufferance.

The card players went into the dining-room for their game. Candlelight was all very well, but it wasn't strong enough to play by, and besides, the breeze was apt to lift the cards from the table. It suited Matthew. It meant Fleur's flirtatious giggle was muted. It also meant he could avoid Lucas's patient face.

Depositing his glass on the tray, he abandoned any thought of pouring himself another drink and crossed the patio. Beyond the low stone wall that formed the boundary of the garden he could hear the gentle murmur of the ocean. Although there was no moonlight to speak of, the lights from the patio illuminated a portion of the beach, and as his eyes became adjusted he could see the curling tide.

It was odd to think that he had never seen the ocean from this angle. Usually he saw the villa from the shoreline, and he remembered the sensation he'd had of being watched. That was how he'd known the villa was occupied. Though he hadn't known by whom until Fleur arrived.

Stepping down on to the softer sand that had drifted against the boundary wall, Matthew kicked off his leather loafers. It was one of the advantages of living in a hot climate that he didn't have to wear socks, and the coral grains were pleasantly cool between his toes.

Tying the laces of his shoes together, he looped them around his neck and walked lazily towards the water. Soon he had left the softer going behind, and the damp sand, compacted by the ocean, was firm beneath his feet. When he'd first come here, he had often used to bathe by moonlight. The idea of being able to swim as nature intended had been a novelty. But these days he generally confined himself to the simpler delights of the pool.

All the same, there was still something rather appealing about stripping off his clothes and wading naked into the waves. It would certainly ease his frustration, he thought wryly. A good cold shower was just what he needed.

Which was ridiculous, he had to admit. It wasn't as if the Graham woman was particularly attractive, after all. Oh, she was tall and slim, and she had nice eyes— but so what? That description could apply to a dozen other women of his acquaintance, and none of them disturbed his concentration.

The water seeped around his toes as he stood there, and he knew he should roll the cuffs of his trousers up. But what the hell? he mused with some impatience. It wasn't as if he cared what anyone else thought.

And then he saw her.

She was coming out of the sea, perhaps fifty yards further along the beach, and for a moment he half believed that his thoughts had conjured her up. In that first, gut-wrenching awareness he thought that she was naked. And then, as he gazed like some dumbstruck youth, he realised that her dress was plastered to her body.

But she had been in the sea, that much was obvious, and, like him, she apparently hadn't cared what happened to her clothes. The skirt of the thin garment was sodden, and she bent to squeeze the hem as she stepped on to the damp sand.

Matthew swallowed, his breath escaping in short, uneven bursts. God, there was something almost— pagan—about her. Had she any idea he was watching her? Or was she totally immune to his eyes?

In a minute she'd be gone, and because this whole scene had all the unreality of a dream, Matthew found himself moving towards her. Perhaps he was imagining it; perhaps she wasn't really there. She was certainly the stuff of fantasy as she rubbed those long, sexy legs.

'Hi.'

His greeting caught her unawares; he knew that immediately. But at least she was all too disturbingly human as she turned her head towards him. Despite the poor light, he was instantly aware that she was no fantasy. Her warmth, her breath, her nearness assaulted his senses. He wanted to reach out and touch her to prove she knew it, too.

Of course, he didn't do any such thing. But he couldn't prevent his eyes from making a swift inventory of her body. Her breasts were far too provocative in profile, and the folds of her dress, clinging to her hips and thighs, were almost more erotic than if she'd been completely naked.

The shadows they created at knee and groin tormented him. He wanted to peel away the fabric and expose the flesh beneath. He wanted to put his hand between her legs, and feel her sweetness. He wanted to feel her close about him and lose all control . . .

'What do you want?' she asked, arresting his descent into madness, and Matthew forced his brain to function over the dictates of his sex. 'I thought you were playing cards,' she added, crossing her arms about her waist almost protectively.

'Well, as you can see, I'm not,' said Matthew evenly, relieved to find that his voice was only marginally affected by his mood. 'Tell me——' he endeavoured to strike a casual tone '—do you usually go swimming fully clothed?'

He thought she might have flushed, but the darkness revealed nothing but a faint glimmer in her eyes. 'Not usually,' she replied tightly. 'I was—hot, that's all. And I didn't want to disturb the children by getting changed.'

Matthew's mouth turned down. 'I thought you said you were going to check on them,' he reminded her smoothly, and she straightened her spine.

'I was. I did. But—they were restless.' She lifted her shoulders. 'I expect they could hear the strange voices. The villa's walls are quite thin.'

'Mmm.' Matthew doubted that had been her motive, but it wasn't worth arguing over. 'It's funny,' he said, 'I was just thinking of doing the same thing. Oh—not plunging in with all my clothes on. But taking a swim.'

Helen's eyes widened. 'Here?'

She sounded quite appalled, and Matthew took his cue. 'Why not?' he asked. 'You've obviously enjoyed it.' He hesitated only a second before flicking the curve of one alluring breast with his finger. 'Was it cold? Is that why...?'

His meaning was obvious, and he could tell by the way her eyes sparked that she resented his familiarity. 'Why don't you find out?' she demanded, swinging round on him unexpectedly, and before he could guess her intentions she'd thrust both hands at his chest.

She was quite strong, he thought, but it wasn't her strength that defeated him. The element of surprise was what caused his downfall. That and a sudden depression of sand beneath his heel.

He tried to regain his balance, but the tide was working in her favour. The undertow sucked away his footing, and with an almighty splash he floundered on to his back.

God, it was cold—or perhaps he had just been incredibly hot. Whatever, the shock of it drove the breath from his lungs, and left him gasping for air. Like some wallowing sea creature, he struggled to regain stability, splashing about and soaking himself with every move he made.

It was her laughter that provoked him into action. Peal after peal of it broke over him as she stood there, apparently forgetting how vulnerable she was. It was as if she thought his position was irretrievable, and only when he scrambled to his feet did she take off.

But she was too late—too late and too slow, and hampered by the soaking folds of her skirt. Matthew's trousers were much less cumbersome, his legs much swifter. He lunged for her ankle without compunction, and wrestled her to the sand.

She was breathless, as much from the laughter his plight had evoked as from her belated sprint across the beach. She fell, a helpless victim to his superior strength, still choking on convulsive giggles as he rolled her on to her back.

'Beast,' she exclaimed, but it came out as a stutter as she tried frantically to crawl away from his hands. Thankfully, the sand was damp, or they'd have both been covered in it, and it squelched beneath his knees as he brought her down.

She was twisting and turning so much that he had to use his weight to subdue her. Even so, she wriggled increasingly under him, trying to draw up her knee between his legs. In the end, he forced her legs apart and lay between them, suffering the jab of her heels against his thighs.

'You didn't honestly expect to get away with it, did you?' he demanded, imprisoning her wrists above her head with one hand, and forcing her to look at him with the other. 'Dammit, what am I going to tell the others when I get back there? They're going to think I'm crazy or something worse.'

They were nearer the terrace now, and the faint illumination spilling from the lanterns caught the fleeting look of withdrawal in her eyes. But it was only a momentary aberration before she answered him. 'You should have thought of that before you made a pass at me,' she retorted. 'Now, will you get off me, you neolithic brute? It's not my fault if you've got some awkward explanations to make.'

'Isn't it?' Matthew made the obvious rejoinder, but he found he was enjoying himself too much to let her go. Beneath his chest her heart was pounding frantically, and a hot surge of awareness was pooling in his groin. His voice thickened. 'Who else's?'

'It's your own fault,' she panted, his weight causing a constriction in her lungs. 'But don't worry. I'm sure your—your sister-in-law will believe you. She's sure to think it was me if you play nice.'

Matthew's eyes narrowed. 'What's that supposed to mean?'

'Nothing.'

Her reply was swift, but he had the impression she'd said more than she intended. Dammit, she couldn't be jealous of Fleur, could she? The implications of that possibility made his head swim.

He looked down at her suddenly, and the eyes that had been wide and imploring a moment ago were quickly veiled. Long lashes, several shades darker than her hair, made a dusky fringe against her cheeks, and for the first time he noticed the tinge of darkness that created a revealing shadow beneath their rims.

Either the children were keeping her awake, or she wasn't sleeping well for some reason, he decided. There was exhaustion in her pallor, and he wanted to know why. But, for the moment, he was selfish enough to put a hold on his compassion. Holding her like this, feeling her move against him, inspired thoughts of a totally different nature. He still wanted to comfort her, but in a very different way.

'You don't have to be jealous of Fleur,' he said, releasing her wrists to cup her face. 'She won't be staying long.'

Her outrage was evident in the violent thrust she made against him, but this time she didn't have a hope in hell of succeeding, he reflected smugly. Her anger only made him even more determined; her frustration made him settle even more surely against her. If she did but know it, she was exciting him by her actions. He could already feel the ache of longing between his legs.

'I don't give a damn how long that woman is staying,' she seethed, but her denial turned to a muffled moan beneath his lips. Giving in to the desire to taste her, his mouth cut off her angry protest, and although she fought his possession she couldn't win.

Groaning his satisfaction, Matthew moved over her, subduing her flailing hands without too much effort. She tried to clench her lips together, but he wouldn't let her, and his tongue entwined with hers in an intimate dance.

He knew the moment when she stopped resisting him. Until then, despite his efforts, it had been a fairly one-sided affair. Her eyes were open and she stared at him in accusation. The sounds she uttered were protests that he ignored.

But suddenly, as if in spite of herself he'd touched some vulnerable chord inside her, she gave in. Almost innocently, it seemed, she surrendered to the sensual brush of his tongue. Her lips parted to allow his hot invasion; when his tongue seared across hers she met its fire with her own.

Her hands, which had been balled against her sides, slid into his hair now. Her nails raked his scalp as he deepened the kiss. She was heat and light and fire, and his blood responded, thickening to a throbbing mass as she arched beneath his thighs.

Did she know what she was doing? he wondered unsteadily, finding it difficult to think coherently with her passion beneath his hands. She was more, so much more than he had ever expected, and his own senses were reeling in eager response.

Her small breasts thrust against his chest, unbearably provocative in his present state of arousal. The wetness of their clothes was creating an urgent friction, and when he released her mouth to take a breath, his eyes dropped to the sensuous suction of their bodies.

He wanted to tear her clothes from her, he thought crazily. He wanted to strip off his own shirt and trousers, and warm her with his heat. But, for all his whirling senses, he knew they were far too close to the villa to allow such madness. He contented himself with lowering his head, and suckling her through the cloth.

Fire shot through him as he took that pert nipple between his lips. For all that its dusky peak was hidden beneath her dress, it tasted like the sweetest kind of heaven. Thrusting, throbbing, it surged into his mouth, and, forgetting what he'd thought a moment before, he gave in to his instincts and unbuttoned her bodice.

Her breasts looked every bit as delicious as they had tasted. Tight and swollen, their pointed fullness tipped towards his mouth, and he took a moment to enjoy their provocation. His own body throbbed in anticipation, and he wondered if she could feel his urgent response. Between his legs his sex was aching, straining for a satisfaction she could give him.

He didn't delay any longer. Although her eyes had barely fluttered when he drew back from her, he was afraid she might suddenly change her mind. But when he took the knotted curve of her breast into his mouth, she barely shuddered. The sigh of contentment that escaped her was an involuntary admission.

Matthew groaned then, low in his throat, the sounds she was making intensifying his need. He wanted her, he thought shakenly. God, he wanted her so much it hurt. He was harder than he'd ever thought possible, and he couldn't hold out much longer.

Her hands slid inside his collar, cool against his spine. Small palms massaged his shoulders, peeling the shirt away from him, as she nuzzled his throat with her tongue. She was tasting him, he thought weakly, feeling that sensuous wetness against his skin. She must know how he was feeling. God, he was perilously near the brink.

A feeling of reckless hunger swept over him. Images of how slick and tight her womanly sheath would be filled his head. He could imagine the fulfilling sweetness of his possession. He could imagine burying himself deep inside her, stretching her to the limits, taking her with him to the mindless heights of oblivion...

Reason reasserted itself. It was lust, he told himself savagely, suppressing the urge to slide his hand up her thigh and discover her arousal for himself. The musky scent of her body and his was all around them, and he wouldn't have been human if he hadn't wanted what she could give. It was a long time since he had been with a woman—any woman—and he was horny. He needed the act, but not the complications. Seducing the Sheridans' nanny wouldn't just be foolish, it would be mad.

Yet, when she gripped his neck and brought his mouth back to hers, temptation hovered. His blood felt like liquid fire in his veins. The feel of her toes, caressing now, was almost driving him crazy, but with a muffled oath he let her go, and got unsteadily to his feet.

CHAPTER SEVEN

'WHEN are you waking up, Helen?'

The plaintive cry, accompanied by a persistent tugging at the sheet which was all that covered her, forced Helen to open her eyes. Sophie was standing beside her bed, still in her baby-doll pyjamas, her thumb tucked unhappily into her mouth.

Helen stifled a groan and blinked rapidly, trying to clear the sleep from her eyes. There was a heavy sense of apprehension hanging over her, which she couldn't quite interpret at this moment, and her head was throbbing dully, as if she'd slept too long.

'Oh, Sophie,' she said, struggling to focus on her watch. 'What time is it?'

'It's late,' replied Sophie defensively, making snuffling noises with her thumb. 'Mummy said I could come and wake you up. She says she's got a headache.'

Haven't we all? thought Helen with some resignation, rolling on to her back. For heaven's sake, what time was it? Tricia didn't usually surface before she did.

When she finally made sense of the pointers on her watch, she gave a horrified gasp. It was half-past eight. She could hardly believe it, but she'd slept long past her normal deadline. She'd acclimatised with a vengeance, and Tricia had a right to feel aggrieved.

And then, as she turned to Sophie to tell her she was sorry, the reasons why she had overslept surged over her. Oh, God, she thought, remembering why she had lain awake for several hours the night before, how could she have been so stupid? She'd actually let Matthew Aitken crawl all over her. She'd let the brother of the man who'd destroyed her father's life almost make love to her. And,

83

what was worse, she hadn't stopped him. She'd encouraged him to do it.

'He—len!'

Sophie's protest was more of an angry whine now, as if she sensed Helen wasn't listening to her any more. Helen's eyes might be open, but she wasn't looking at her. She was staring right through her, and Sophie didn't like it.

'What?' With an effort, Helen forced her treacherous thoughts aside and struggled to pay attention. 'Oh—yes, I am late, aren't I?' she said ruefully. 'Go and tell your mummy I won't be long. I must just wash my face.'

'You slept in.' Henry's appearance in the doorway heralded another accusation, and Helen wondered if Tricia realised how like her her son was. 'You're not s'posed to sleep in,' he added reprovingly. 'You're s'posed to give us our breakfast.'

'And I will,' said Helen wearily, 'just as soon as I've cleaned my teeth and got some clothes on. Now——' she forced a smile '—why don't you two do the same? I'm sure you can manage to put your clothes on without me for once.'

'We're not s'posed——' began Henry, but Sophie cut him off.

'I'm staying here,' she declared, depositing herself on the end of Helen's bed. 'I want to watch you get dressed. I can, can't I? I'm a girl.'

'Well——'

'If you're staying, I'm staying,' announced Henry, and Helen pushed aside the sheet with a tired hand.

'You're neither of you staying,' she declared, making sure her nightshirt covered her thighs before swinging her legs out of bed. 'I won't be long, I promise. Now, be good children and go and brush your teeth.'

With the door closed firmly behind them, Helen drew the first unrestrained breath of the day. At least she had a few minutes to recover herself. She had the feeling she was going to need them this morning.

Examining her reflection in the mirror above the bathroom basin, she wasn't surprised to find the shadows around her eyes had deepened. Ever since she'd discovered that her mother was staying on the island she'd had a problem sleeping. But last night—and that encounter with Matthew Aitken—was something else.

Dear God, she thought, smoothing the fine veins below her eyes with the tips of her fingers, why hadn't she just kept out of the way, as she'd intended? Why had she gone for the walk along the beach? And why had she chosen to swim?

It had been such a crazy thing to do. Even now, with the benefit of hindsight, she couldn't honestly say what had driven her into the ocean. She'd been hot, of course, and restless, and her nerves had been taut and strung. But she hadn't intended to ruin her dress by soaking it with salt-water.

Nevertheless, that was what she had done, and until Matthew had come upon her she'd quite enjoyed the freedom to be herself. She'd told herself she wouldn't think about Fleur, wouldn't allow her to ruin this trip. But the trouble was, she'd already done that. Helen was never going to forget she was there.

Even so, Fleur hadn't recognised her. She wouldn't have made that stupid mistake over her name if she had. Giving Matthew a bogus surname had been reckless, of course, but with a bit of luck she might get away with it. She had the feeling they wouldn't be seeing either him or his sister-in-law again after last night. Even without what had happened, Matthew had been bored, and Tricia's attempt to get him to talk about his work had patently annoyed him.

Besides, if the name she'd given was ever questioned, she could always pretend that he had been mistaken. Gregory—Graham—they did sound sufficiently alike to support her theory, and she would like to think that Lucas would defend her.

She sighed. She'd liked Matthew's assistant very much. He'd talked to her a lot as she'd toyed with her supper, and, for all he worked for the enemy, he was one of the nicest men she'd met.

Yet she hadn't treated Matthew Aitken like an enemy, she reminded herself unhappily, unable to keep her humiliating thoughts at bay. For all her proud intentions, she'd given in without a contest, and if he hadn't pushed her away, she'd have let him prove it.

Oh, God!

Pressing her lips together, she stared painfully at her pale, drawn features, but she found no answers in her dry-eyed gaze. Although she wanted to cry, she wouldn't let herself. She wanted nothing to remind Tricia of the night before.

She had hoped she might sneak back to the villa without anyone seeing her, but, as everything else had worked against her that evening, she wasn't really surprised when she didn't make it. By the time she had dragged herself up from the sand, fastened her bodice and squeezed the water from her hem, the card-players had left the table. They were sitting on the veranda when she tried to slide past them and, despite her best efforts, Andrew had seen her.

It appeared, though she had learned this only incidentally, that Lucas was indirectly to blame for her exposure. Apparently he hadn't been able to grasp the rules of bidding, and the game had had to be abandoned.

But her appearance had provided a much more noteworthy topic for conversation, and Helen had had to stand there, feeling like one of her own charges, while Tricia took her to task for leaving the villa. Helen's explanation, that she had gone for a walk and fallen into the ocean, had not been received with any sympathy. It was madness, Tricia had declared, to go walking after dark on her own, and she had appealed to her husband to support her.

Helen had been uncomfortably aware that Andrew Sheridan was more interested in the way her wet skirts clung to her legs, and that her mother was watching her, too, with narrowed eyes. Dear God, she'd thought, she could do without this. And where was Matthew? Had he gone home to change?

In the event, it had been Lucas who'd taken pity on her. Although she suspected he had his own motives for helping her, he had suggested she ought to be allowed to go and dry herself. He'd made some comment about them not wanting their nanny laid up with pneumonia, and the veracity of this statement had rung a chord.

She hadn't returned to the party. For all she'd been curious to know how Matthew was going to explain his absence, she'd remained in her room for the rest of the evening. She'd told herself she didn't want to hear what lies he would tell to excuse himself, but the truth was she was too ashamed to see him again.

It also meant she hadn't had to speak to her mother again. And she supposed that was a blessing in disguise. The woman she remembered bore no resemblance to the brittle creature who'd sat at the Sheridans' table. Yet obviously this was the real Fleur, and not the childhood illusion she recalled.

The children were washed and dressed, and tucking into bowls of Rice Crispies when their mother came into the kitchen. For once Tricia was dressed, but whether that was to endorse the fact that Helen had slept in or because she had other plans, Helen couldn't say.

'Oh, so there you are,' she declared, as if Helen spent her time trying to avoid her. 'I was beginning to wonder if you'd decided to give notice. After last night's little fiasco, there was always a doubt.'

Helen refused to be intimidated, but she looked down at the barely touched croissant on her plate and made a pretence of spreading it with conserve. For all her determination, she didn't trust herself to meet Tricia's eyes without flinching, and the last thing she needed was for her employer to suspect she had something to hide.

'Did you want something, Tricia?' she asked, aware of the children looking on with interest. Henry, particularly, enjoyed any kind of altercation, and even Sophie's eyes were round as she looked at them over her spoon.

'Did I want something?' echoed their mother, and Helen's heart sank at the obvious aggression in her tone. 'I want an explanation, if that's not too much to ask. I assume you know that one of our guests left the party without saying goodbye? I want to know what you said that caused him to push you in the water.'

'Did someone push you in the water, Helen?' exclaimed Henry, his cereal forgotten in his excitement, but Helen had no time to feed his curiosity.

'No one pushed me in the water,' she exclaimed, resentful of the implication. 'I told you what happened: I fell. That's all there is to say.'

'Really?'

Patently Tricia didn't believe her, and Helen thought how ironic it was that the Sheridans had got totally the wrong end of the stick. 'Yes,' she said now. 'How could you think anything different? And—and as for one of your guests—leaving, perhaps you should ask yourself why, not me.'

Tricia gasped. 'What do you mean?'

Helen pressed her lips together. 'Nothing,' she said at last. 'I don't mean anything. But if we're talking about Matthew Aitken, I don't think he was exactly thrilled with the evening.'

'Mmm.' Tricia rested her chin on the knuckles of one hand. 'He wasn't the easiest of supper companions, I will admit. So—you didn't see him again, after we went to play cards.'

'I didn't say that.' Helen couldn't tell an outright lie. Fudging about how she'd got wet—that was prevarication. But if Tricia should ask Matthew, she couldn't be sure of what he might say.

'So you did see him?'

'Briefly.' Helen licked her lips. 'He was going for a walk, I think.' She crossed her fingers in her lap. 'He must have walked home.'

Tricia frowned. 'He didn't say where he was going?'

That was simple. 'No.'

'Was this before or after you—fell into the water?' asked Tricia slyly. Then, 'You know, I can't believe he'd abandon the party like that, in spite of what Fleur had to say.'

Helen stiffened. 'What did she say?'

'Oh, this and that.' Tricia gave her an irritated look. 'She asked where we'd found you, actually. I suppose you're not the usual sort of nanny.'

Helen took a breath. 'I—thought you meant she'd said something about—about Matthew Aitken,' she said, not sure whether she ought to be alarmed about Fleur's interest in her or not. Probably not, she assured herself ruefully. Her mother had only ever been interested in herself.

'Well, she did,' Tricia exclaimed now, rather petulantly. 'She màde some excuse about him getting ideas at the most inconvenient times.' She sighed. 'I suppose I shouldn't have suggested playing bridge, but Fleur was so enthusiastic. She said she'd missed playing awfully since she went to live in the United States. Apparently, her late husband's father breeds horses, and naturally——'

'She said that?' Helen broke in, swallowing convulsively. 'That she'd missed playing bridge since she went to live in Florida?'

'Yes.' Tricia's eyes narrowed. 'But how do you know she lives in Florida? I don't recall her talking to you, and I certainly didn't tell you that.'

Helen felt her colour deepen. 'Oh—well, Lucas must have mentioned it,' she replied hurriedly. She forced herself to remain calm. 'Does it matter? I don't suppose we're likely to see them again.'

'You might not,' said Tricia tartly, 'but I'm sure Drew and I will get an invitation to Dragon Bay. It's only polite, in the circumstances. And Fleur knows how much I'd love to see the house.'

'But it's not her house, is it?' Helen pointed out, and then was relieved when Henry chose to speak. She'd said too much already. She should learn to keep her mouth shut.

'Can we come?' he asked, and for a moment both women looked blank. 'To Dragon Bay,' he added. 'Are there really dragons there? Sophie won't like it if there are.'

'I will, too,' declared his sister, digging him in the ribs, but their mother was in no mood to listen to their bickering.

'Just mind your own business, both of you,' she said. 'And only speak when you're spoken to. This is a private conversation. I'm talking to Helen, not you.'

'But are there dragons?' persisted Sophie, who was always slower than her brother, and her mother gave her a fulminating look.

'Of course there aren't,' she snapped. 'Don't you know when Henry's teasing you? Now, hurry up and finish your breakfast. And stop slurping into your food.'

Sophie's jaw wobbled, and she gave her brother a tearful glare. She usually got the worst of any argument, and Helen thought again how little Tricia understood her own children.

'Anyway,' she continued, just when Helen was beginning to think she'd got away with it, 'for someone who's supposedly not interested in seeing them again, you appear to have asked an awful lot of questions. Which reminds me, what did Matthew Aitken say when you—met him on the beach? I assume you didn't talk about the weather?'

Helen took a breath. Her thoughts were racing wildly, and she cast about for something trite to say. What had they talked about? she wondered. Aside from the sarcastic comment he'd made about her swimming fully clothed, she couldn't remember a thing. The trouble was, it was what he had *done* that was balking her memory. From the moment he'd touched her, it was all as painfully clear as a bell.

'He—we—talked about swimming,' she said at last, realising there was a danger in admitting it, but accepting it was the lesser of two evils. If she refused to answer, Tricia was bound to become suspicious, and making something up was almost as bad.

Liars had to have good memories, she acknowledged unhappily, and dealing with Matthew Aitken was far too fraught. The closer she stuck to the truth, the better. And it wasn't such an unusual topic, after all.

'Swimming?'

The other woman stared at her disbelievingly, but before she could say anything more there was an unholy crash. Helen guessed Sophie had been trying to pay Henry back for teasing her, and, in reaching across the table, she'd sent her dish tumbling to the floor.

The ensuing uproar successfully diverted the conversation away from Helen. Maria came rushing in, declaring that the milk would sink into the tiles and go sour. And Sophie, getting down from her chair, slipped on the mushy cereal. Somehow she cut her leg on a shard of china, and because it had started to bleed she began to scream.

It was too much for Tricia. 'Oh, for heaven's sake,' she exclaimed, looking disgustedly at her daughter, before leaving them to deal with the mess without her. And, although Helen wouldn't have wished Sophie hurt for the world, she couldn't help being grateful for small mercies.

'Will I still be able to go in the water?' asked Sophie later, sniffing into a tissue as Helen applied a strip of plaster to her thigh. 'You said we could play in the rockpools today, didn't you? I've got my bucket and spade all ready.'

'Your bucket and spade,' scoffed Henry, hands in pockets, watching the proceedings with a jaundiced eye, but Helen ignored him.

'I think we'll just do a little fishing with our nets this morning,' she declared, half wishing she'd never suggested going on to the beach now. They were too accessible there, too vulnerable. And although, after what had happened the night before, she didn't flatter herself that Matthew Aitken would want to see her, she'd no wish to reinforce his impression that she was easy.

Easy!

Oh, God! Straightening from her task, Helen got to her feet with a heavy heart. How had it happened? she wondered. How had she got herself into such a situation? It simply wasn't like her. She'd always considered herself so self-contained before. Naturally, she'd had men-friends. In fact, one man had actually got as far as asking her to marry him about two years ago. But she'd been quite content living with her father. And, although she'd expected to get married one day, she'd certainly been in no hurry.

Was in no hurry now, she appended, remembering that even in the depths of her despair she'd never considered taking that way out. Marrying someone just to provide herself with financial support had never been an option. In fact lately, since she'd come to work for the Sheridans, she'd begun to wonder if marriage was so desirable after all. Living with someone had to be easier. And, best of all, it kept your options open.

Last night must have been an aberration, she decided. She simply wasn't the type to act that way. She was exaggerating what had happened and punishing herself needlessly. For heaven's sake, the man had only kissed her. It was no big deal.

And yet, remembering how mindlessly abandoned she'd felt when he moved over her, it wasn't quite so easy to dismiss the whole affair. He hadn't only kissed her, he'd touched her intimately. And she'd wanted him to do it. She'd wanted him to do more...

'Why are you looking so cross, Helen?'

Sophie was gazing up at her with her thumb in her mouth, a sure sign that she wasn't totally convinced she hadn't done something wrong, and Helen forced herself to smile at her.

'I'm not looking cross,' she denied, not altogether truthfully. 'I'm just thinking, that's all. I believe I saw some shrimp nets in the cupboard, that the Parrish children must have left behind. Why don't we take them with us? You never know what we might find.'

'Which cupboard?' exclaimed Henry, proving he wasn't wholly immune to the delights of the beach, and Sophie pushed herself in front of him indignantly.

'I'll get them,' she said. 'Where are they, Helen? And I'll need my bucket, won't I? To put the fishes in.'

'Fish,' said Helen firmly, stopping Henry from pinching his sister's bottom, and giving him a reproving stare. 'We'll need the buckets to collect the fish. Well— the crabs and tiny molluscs we're likely to find in the rockpools.'

'What are moll—molluscs?' asked Henry with difficulty, but Helen just ushered him out of the door.

'I'll tell you when we find some,' she said. 'And I'll get the nets myself. I suggest you get your bucket, unless you want to be left out.'

With both children wearing hats, and their still pink limbs liberally coated with sun-blocking cream, Helen shepherded her charges on to the beach. Happily, from her point of view, it was completely deserted, and after dropping their towels in a prominent place she escorted them down to the nearest cluster of rocks.

The pools were warm, and for all her earlier apprehension Helen soon found she was enjoying herself. It reminded her of holidays she had spent with her father when she was a child. He had had endless patience with her, and it couldn't have been easy being a single parent in those days. Of course, she had had a nanny, too, but, unlike Henry and Sophie, she hadn't been abandoned to her own resources. Whenever possible James Gregory had looked after his daughter himself, and it was this that had created the bond between them that she'd found so hard to let go.

'Oooh, what's that?' asked Sophie, grimacing, and skipping out of the water as a weird-looking creature emerged from the shade of the rocks. Even Henry got out of the way as its spiny shell turned in his direction, and, recognising it as a sea-urchin, Helen scooped it out of the water.

'Not to be touched,' she said decisively, shaking it out of the net into another pool some distance away. 'Those spines can dig into your toes, and it hurts when you try to get them out.'

'Ugh.' Sophie gave a theatrical shiver, and Helen thought it had been a salutary lesson for them all. They weren't on the beach at Bournemouth, and for all its beauty this paradise did have one or two unpleasant inhabitants.

'I wasn't afraid,' declared Henry, brave after the event, and Helen gave him an old-fashioned look.

'Then I'll get you to deal with the next one we see,' she said pleasantly, and smiled as he looked anxiously about him.

Notwithstanding the heat, and the ever-present danger of the children falling over and hurting themselves, Helen found herself relaxing. Away from the house, and with no disturbing neighbour on the horizon, she could almost convince herself that nothing bad had happened. Even the thought of her mother, sunning herself on Matthew's veranda, only aroused a muted resentment. Despite the shock she'd had, she'd lived for almost twenty years without seeing her mother, and she had to be pragmatic if she wanted to keep her job.

Because they never stayed out too long, in a short while Helen peeled off her shorts and T-shirt and took them down to the water's edge. She reasoned that salt-water was unlikely to cause Sophie any problems, and it was so good to feel the comparative coolness on her skin after the undiluted heat of the sun.

Both children wanted to swim, but Helen didn't let them go out of their depth. For all it looked so idyllic, the current was quite strong. Henry grumbled, as usual, but he was still wary of finding another sea urchin, and Sophie splashed about quite happily in the shallows.

She was so busy keeping tabs on both children, however, that she wasn't aware of anyone's approach

until a woman spoke. And, because Henry and Sophie
only stared at the visitor, Helen guessed who it was before
she turned her head.

'Hello, Miss—Graham?'

Her mother was alone. Helen hadn't expected her to
be, and she'd already steeled herself to meet Matthew's
mocking gaze when she turned around. But only Fleur
was standing there, looking like an exotic butterfly in
billowing silk trousers and a poncho-like top of flowing
chiffon. She was wearing dark glasses, too, which made
her expression hard to read. But the fact that she was
here at all caused a sudden sinking in Helen's stomach.

Oh, lord, she thought, grasping Henry's and Sophie's
hands and drawing them closer, as if in protection. Did
Fleur know who she was? Was that why she had come?

CHAPTER EIGHT

MATTHEW woke up with a hangover.

It wasn't the first time it had happened, and he didn't imagine it would be the last, but it was frustrating. He didn't enjoy working with a pounding head, and he wasn't in a particularly good temper when he stepped into the shower.

It was late, too, he noticed. It must have been after nine before he stirred. Too late for a walk, too late to go jogging; his whole schedule had been messed up. He preferred to be at his desk by nine o'clock and no later. He'd be lucky if he made it by ten the way things were going.

Not that it really mattered, he acknowledged edgily as he stood beneath the pummelling spray. It wasn't as if he had a deadline, or an editor breathing down his neck for copy. But he'd always believed it was essential to have self-discipline, particularly if, like he did, you worked for yourself.

It was a habit he had acquired during his days as a roving correspondent. Not that he'd had a desk to sit at in those days, but the discipline had been just as important. That was why he had been successful; why he had been on the spot when some of his fellow journalists had still been recovering from the previous night's excesses. Wherever he'd been, whatever he'd done—and he had to admit he had been as wild as any of them when he was younger—he'd always been around when he was needed.

Which was hardly a description of what had happened last night, he brooded angrily. He'd been on the spot all right, but it wasn't a memory he wanted to keep. Looking back, the whole affair had all the elements of fantasy. He didn't know what had possessed him; he could hardly believe how reckless he had been.

And the fact that that was the real reason why he had a hangover this morning was what was really bugging him. As soon as he'd opened his aching eyes, he'd remembered. God Almighty, he was too old to go cavorting about on the beach like some sex-starved adolescent; too old to arrive back at the villa soaked to the skin and howling with frustration.

Of course, he'd resorted to the only refuge he knew. By the time Fleur and Lucas came home, he was past feeling anything at all. Which was just as well, he reflected, turning off the shower. He hated to think he'd been so desperate that he might have turned to Fleur for comfort. Perhaps he was flattering himself, but he feared that was exactly why she was here.

He half expected Lucas to appear as he was dressing. They often discussed work, or the day's mail, before he returned to his study. But, like everything else this morning, his expectations didn't run to order. Lucas was sitting at the breakfast table, staring broodingly into space, when he entered the room.

A plate of scrambled eggs was congealing in front of him, and, judging by the almost-empty state of the coffee-pot, Matthew guessed the other man wasn't feeling like eating either. Still, at least he was alone, he thought with some relief. As only one place had been disturbed, it appeared that Fleur was still in bed.

'Hi,' he said, when Lucas only offered him a silent acknowledgement. For all he wasn't feeling in the mood to be conciliatory, he guessed Lucas was peeved because he'd abandoned them the night before. And, what the hell, it wasn't his assistant's fault that he'd behaved like an idiot. He deserved an explanation, but Matthew was loath to tell the truth.

Lucas's brows arched. 'Hi,' he conceded, after a moment. Then, with some enjoyment, 'You look like hell.'

'Thanks.' Matthew hooked out a chair and levered himself into it. 'I'll return the compliment some time.'

Lucas's expression wilted. 'Well,' he muttered, as if in vindication, 'that was a rotten trick you pulled last night. Do you have any idea what it was like, trying to mollify the Sheridans? Making excuses when there weren't any to make.'

Matthew pulled a wry face. 'I'm sorry.'

'So you should be.' Lucas warmed to his theme. 'It was bloody embarrassing, I can tell you. I don't often give Fleur any credit, but I have to admit, she saved your neck.'

Matthew's mouth turned down. 'Really?'

'Yes, really.' Lucas pushed the eggs aside, and poured himself the last dregs of the coffee. 'She made up some tale about you getting these sudden ideas, that had to be immediately recorded in case you forgot them. She assured those poor sods that you'd be working at your word processor until all hours.' He grimaced. 'Whether they believed her is another story, if you'll forgive the pun.'

Matthew scowled. 'Does it matter?'

'It does to me.' Lucas glared back. 'Until you had that clever idea of me playing cards instead of you, Helen and I were getting along nicely. She's a really interesting woman, Matt, and I'd hoped to see her again.'

Matthew suppressed the sudden surge of emotion he felt at hearing the other man talk about Helen so familiarly. He told himself it was irritation; he refused to consider that it might be anything else. For God's sake, she was just a little tramp, he thought repressively. He didn't care about her. It was Lucas he was thinking about. He didn't want his friend to get hurt.

All the same, he couldn't quite hide the rancour in his voice as he answered him. 'In what way was she interesting?' he asked. 'Whenever I looked in your direction, you seemed to be doing all the talking.'

Lucas flushed then, and Matthew felt even worse. He had enough guilt rolling round inside him already. Did he have to make fun of the other man just to satisfy his own perverted sense of justice?

'I admit—I did do most of the talking,' Lucas conceded now. 'But that was just because we didn't have enough time together. If you hadn't cut and run, I might have learned something more about her. I know I said she was only here for a month, but, hell—a month can seem like a lifetime.'

'Can't it just,' murmured Matthew drily. And then, as another thought occurred to him, 'She—er—she did go back to the party, didn't she?'

'Go back?' Lucas pounced on the words, and Matthew hurried to rectify his mistake.

'Well—yes,' he said. 'I—er—I met her on the beach. When I was walking back,' he added. 'I—think she'd been in the water.'

Lucas frowned. 'I wonder why she didn't say she'd seen you?' he mused. 'Still, as you say, she was wet.' His eyes narrowed. 'You had nothing to do with that, I suppose?'

'No.' Matthew made the denial without hesitation. 'As I said before, she was wet before she saw me. Perhaps she'd been swimming. People have done crazier things.'

Lucas shook his head. 'She said she'd fallen. In the water, I mean. But, as you say, who knows? In any event, she went off to change and didn't come back. Fleur and I had a couple of drinks, and then we came home.'

Matthew inclined his head, annoyed that he couldn't find anything in Lucas's story to lift his mood. Last night had proved to him that getting involved with Helen Graham would be madness. He didn't need that kind of complication in his life.

Ruth appeared just then, to ask him if he wanted his usual breakfast, but this morning he refused everything but toast and coffee. He needed the caffeine to alleviate his headache, and a slice of toast might help to calm the churning in his gut.

'So,' he said, after the housekeeper had gone, forcing himself to be civil. 'Where's my dear sister-in-law this morning? Not that I'm worried,' he added swiftly. 'I just like to keep ahead of the game.'

Lucas grimaced. 'She's gone out.'

'Out?' Matthew stared at him disbelievingly. 'Fleur's gone out alone? I don't believe it.'

'Oh, it's true,' Lucas assured him. 'I saw her leaving the garden myself. She seemed to be heading towards Dragon Point. Perhaps she enjoyed the Sheridans' company better than we thought?'

Matthew's stomach tightened. 'You're not serious!'

'Why not?'

Why not, indeed? Matthew didn't really understand the sense of apprehension he was feeling himself. He just doubted Fleur had gone to Dragon Point to see the Sheridans. It wasn't in Fleur's nature to cultivate anyone she couldn't use.

And yet, why else would she go there? Not to see Helen, he was sure. Unless he'd said or done something to make her think he was interested in the younger woman. Despite the unwelcome implications of that thought, he wouldn't like to see the girl terrorised by Fleur.

Unable to sit still with such thoughts churning his already queasy stomach, Matthew thrust back his chair and got unsteadily to his feet. Dammit, what was he going to do? He could hardly go charging after her like some latter-day cavalier.

'What's the matter?'

Lucas was looking at him curiously, and, realising he was acting out of character, Matthew pulled a rueful face. 'Too much to drink, I guess,' he said, squeezing the back of his neck and finding it clammy. 'And I'm not sure I trust Fleur. What the hell is she playing at?'

Lucas frowned. 'Well, I must admit I wondered where she was going,' he conceded. 'D'you want me to go after her? She hasn't been gone long.'

Matthew hesitated, as though giving the matter some thought. 'No,' he said at last, as if coming to a decision. 'I need some air myself. I'll go see what she's doing.'

*   *   *

'Is the water cold?'

Fleur stood safely out of reach of the incoming tide, her high-heeled sandals totally unsuitable for a walk along the beach. She had to keep moving to prevent her heels from sinking into the sand, and Helen doubted the salt would improve the expensive bronze leather.

But, with the children waiting to see what she would say, she was obliged to answer her mother. 'It's—quite warm, actually,' she replied politely. But she was under no illusions that Fleur's enquiry meant that she wanted to join them.

'I never liked swimming in the sea,' she declared now, making sure the creamy rivulets didn't reach her feet. 'Salt-water dries your skin, and the sand gets into everything. I hated that gritty feeling between my toes.'

'I like it,' said Sophie, letting go of Helen's hand and paddling out of the water. She splashed a bit, and Fleur stifled an impatient exclamation. But she didn't go away as Helen had hoped.

Henry hunched his shoulders and scowled at Helen. 'Who is she?' he asked in a stage whisper. 'What does she want?'

'Oh——' Helen bit her lip. 'Um—this is Mrs Aitken, Henry. You remember: she came to supper with Mummy and Daddy last evening. She's staying at the house beyond the headland.'

'Where the dragons are?' asked Sophie at once, and Helen wished they'd stayed in the garden after all.

'It's called Dragon Bay,' said Fleur, keeping well away from danger. 'But there aren't any dragons. Who on earth told you there were?'

'Maybe you're a dragon,' said Henry rudely, responding to the edge of contempt in the woman's tone. 'And how do you know there aren't any dragons? You don't live there.'

'He has a point,' drawled another voice, a male one this time, and Helen wondered what she'd done to deserve this fate. She'd been so busy worrying about something that wasn't going to happen, she'd overlooked the very thing that had.

'Oh, Matt!'

For all she was sure that her mother had expected this, Helen glimpsed a trace of impatience in Fleur's eyes as she turned to her brother-in-law. Just for a moment, she had the feeling that Fleur was as shocked to see him as she was, but it might have been because of what he'd said.

'Good morning,' he said now, encompassing all of them in the greeting, and Helen decided that this was her chance to escape. Without looking at him at all, she offered a muffled greeting, and then shepherded the children before her up the beach.

'My bucket—I've forgotten my bucket,' protested Sophie loudly, and, adjuring the children to stay where they were, Helen ran back to get it. She was not unaware that, in her green- and white-striped bikini, she was at something of a disadvantage, but she snatched up the bucket quickly, and turned to make her escape.

'I hope we haven't spoiled your plans for the morning,' Matthew remarked drily, and she was forced to acknowledge him then, or arouse her mother's suspicions.

'Not at all,' she said stiffly, clutching the bucket to her midriff. 'We never stay out long. It's much too hot for the children.'

'For you, too, by the look of it,' he commented, and she wondered if he was being deliberately unkind because Fleur was looking on.

She didn't need him to tell her that her face was like a lobster. She was burning with humiliation inside as well as out.

'Don't be cruel, Matt.' Her mother came to her rescue, but once again Helen sensed she had her own reasons for doing so. 'Come along, darling. We've taken up enough of Miss—Graham's time.'

'If you'll excuse me...'

Helen just wanted to get as far away as possible—from both of them. It seemed obvious to her that whatever Matthew Aitken had said there was something going on between them. It sickened her, not just because of who Fleur was, but because of her own vulnerability. In God's name, why had she let him touch her?

The image of his dark, sardonic face accompanied her back to the house. That, and the unwelcome memory of Fleur clinging on to his arm. He had strong arms, dark-skinned and muscular, covered with a light coating of dusky hair, just like his legs.

Andrew was just coming out on to the patio as they reached the house, and he viewed her half-naked state with obviously appreciative eyes. 'Well, well,' he said. 'Nurse's uniforms get better all the time.' He grinned at Helen's discomfort. 'You appear to have caught the sun.'

'We saw Mr and Mrs Aitken,' declared Sophie, evidently assuming Fleur's familiarity with Matthew meant they were married. Relationships were always simple in the little girl's mind, and Helen stifled a sigh when Andrew frowned.

'Mr and Mrs Aitken?' he echoed. 'Would that be Fleur and Matthew Aitken?'

'Who else?' replied Helen, heading for the children's bedroom. 'Come along, you two. Let's go and take a shower.'

'Can I come?' asked their father, in an undertone only she could hear, and Helen hoped Andrew was not going to prove a nuisance on this holiday. The little she'd seen of him in London had not led her to believe he might become a problem, but since his arrival three days ago she'd been on her guard.

There'd been that business at the airport, for example. And while Helen knew it had just been a game on his part, she'd been left with the feeling that Andrew liked to tease. With her mother to contend with, she didn't need any more problems. She half wished they could just pack up and go home.

The rest of the day passed reasonably uneventfully. To Helen's relief, Tricia took her husband off to have lunch with some friends in Bridgetown, and after their afternoon nap both Henry and Sophie were disposed to be friendly. She suspected it was the heat as much as anything that was sapping their energy, and they were quite content to splash about in the swimming-pool, which was partially shaded by a stand of palms.

The Sheridans didn't come back until after six, and by then Helen had the children bathed and ready for bed. She'd eaten her evening meal with them, to avoid having to join her employers, and she spent the evening reading, and trying to come to terms with what she should do.

Now that she was certain that Fleur was her mother, it had put her into something of a quandary. For all she told herself that her mother had deserted her, that she owed her nothing, the ties of blood couldn't be wholly ignored. Whatever she felt about Fleur, however much she resented the fact that she'd been thrust into her orbit, the fact remained that it had happened. Could she just forget about her? Or did she owe it to her father's memory to tell her mother who she was?

It would be hard explaining why she'd lied about her surname to Matthew, of course. Would Fleur believe that it had just been a knee-jerk reaction, brought about by her initial desire to hide her identity from her? She couldn't deny the panic that had gripped her when she'd first been faced with the woman. Was that why she'd succumbed to Matthew's lovemaking? Because she'd already used up all her resistance with Fleur?

It was too simplistic a solution, of course. The truth was, she didn't know why it had happened. She'd been distressed, perhaps, but hardly incoherent. Yet, when Matthew had laid his hands upon her, she'd melted like jelly in his arms.

And, unhappily, that had complicated an already complicated situation. Yet her involvement with him had started even before she'd recognised her mother. From the moment he'd accosted her at the airport, she'd been aware of him as a man. It was crazy, because he'd made it perfectly obvious he found her foolish. Beyond stripping her of her dignity—among other things—he'd just treated her with contempt. He was probably like his brother, she thought unhappily. He didn't care about anyone else's feelings but his own.

The thing she didn't want to think about was what his relationship with her mother might be. For all she and her father had lived a fairly free and easy existence, because she had been with him so much she was pitiably ignorant when it came to men like Matthew. Her own experience told her he probably didn't have a conscience, and if Fleur needed another protector, she could probably do a lot worse.

She half regretted not having supper with the Sheridans later, when she lay awake for hours, wishing the dawn would come. A couple of glasses of wine might have solved her sleeping problem, and it didn't help that she could hear Tricia and Andrew arguing through the thin walls of their bedroom.

Eventually she did sleep, however, though this time she awakened in good time to get the children's breakfasts. Despite her disturbed night, she felt reasonably rested, and she reflected that it sometimes happened that way. The previous day she'd overslept, and she'd felt heavy-eyed all morning.

It was after seven, however, when she opened the shutters and stepped out on to the veranda. Long after she might have expected to see Matthew, she acknowledged with some relief. She hadn't asked him if he'd seen her, but as she'd seen him it was always possible. She wouldn't like him to think she was haunting him. After what had happened, she'd be wiser to keep her distance.

Nevertheless, she couldn't deny a sudden mental image of her mother and Matthew in bed together. Brown skin on pale flesh; straight dark hair mingling with silvery blonde curls. A hairy leg wedged between two pearl-pale thighs... Dear God, she thought in horror, what in

heaven's name was happening to her? She'd never had
thoughts like these before she'd met that man.

Henry and Sophie were less amiable this morning.
Some time during the night Henry had hidden Matilda,
so Helen had to spend most of the time before breakfast
looking for the rag doll. Of course, Henry said he hadn't
touched it, but Sophie didn't believe him, and after
finding the doll hidden beneath the little girl's mattress
Helen didn't believe him either.

Consequently, they were late getting their showers, and
late turning up for breakfast. Much to Helen's dismay,
the children's father was already at the table, and she
had to spend the meal parrying his teasing, which became
increasingly personal.

'Your father was a yachtsman, wasn't he?' Andrew
said idly, as Helen was about to usher the children out
of the door. 'I'm thinking of renting a sailboat. Can I
count on you to crew for me?'

'Oh——' Helen licked her lips, as much disturbed by
his thoughtless question as by the implications it evoked.
'I—don't think I'm much good, actually. My father often
sailed alone. I was never very keen.'

Which was another lie, she thought unhappily, wondering if being a forecourt attendant at a petrol station
wouldn't have been less troublesome after all. It was all
very well congratulating herself on the success of her
relationship with the children, but nobody had warned
her that her relationship with the parents might require
a degree in social studies.

'Mmm.'

She had the feeling Andrew didn't believe her, but she
hoped, if he mentioned the matter to Tricia, that her
erstwhile friend might understand her reluctance to get
involved. It had been tactless to mention her father, particularly in connection with sailing, and if her motives
were more personal, Tricia was not to know.

Although she was loath to take the children on to the
beach again, the idea of staying by the pool, and perhaps
being dragged into another of the Sheridans' arguments,

didn't give her much of a choice. Besides, she doubted they would encounter the Aitkens a second time. A coincidence was a coincidence, but once was surely enough.

The children had brought their buckets and spades, and Helen spent the first half-hour helping Henry construct a castle. He had very definite ideas of how high he wanted it to be, and where they should put the moat, and keeping Sophie from jeopardising the project took all her concentration.

Nevertheless, some sixth sense seemed to alert her the moment Fleur appeared from the belt of palms that fringed the end of the beach. Once again, her mother was alone, and the connotations of that circumstance couldn't be ignored. She had to have a reason for coming here, whether Matthew had aborted the purpose of yesterday's visit or not. Helen's nerves tightened unpleasantly, but there was no way she could avoid the woman's presence.

'It's Mrs Aitken,' cried Sophie, being less interested in the castle and therefore more easily diverted. She looked at Helen. 'D'you think she's come to see us?'

'I doubt it.' Helen tried to be casual, merely casting the woman a polite smile before continuing with her task. 'Henry, pass me that shell, will you? I need to shore up the sides of the gateway.'

'Good morning.'

Fleur was evidently determined to create as much disruption as possible, and Henry looked up at her with a critical frown. 'We're making a castle,' he said. 'Do you want to help us? We need someone to fetch the water, and Sophie always spills it.'

'No, I don't.'

'Yes, you do.'

The children started one of their usual pointless arguments, and Helen, who could see the half-built castle coming to a sorry end, got automatically to her feet. Henry was pushing Sophie now, and she was trying to retaliate, stepping all over his carefully laid foundations, and wringing a cry of anguish from her brother.

Helen moved to separate them, glad she hadn't shed her T-shirt and shorts as she'd done the previous day. Her mother, cool and elegant in flowing lemon trousers and a long silk sweater, was watching the proceedings with a resigned expression, her pale eyes hidden as before beneath a pair of dark glasses.

'Leave them to it,' Fleur said carelessly, and Helen thought how incongruous it had been of Henry to ask her to join them. The idea of Fleur fetching water or helping Henry build his castle was ludicrous. Helen doubted she'd ever been that kind of mother. Even when she was young. She was more at home beside a swimming-pool than braving the ravages of the beach.

So why was she here?

'Can we talk?' Fleur added quietly, glancing rather apprehensively about her. 'I'm sure these two can amuse themselves for five minutes, if we just saunter down to the ocean.'

Helen held up her head. 'Why should I want to saunter down to the ocean with you?' she asked tersely. 'We hardly know one another.'

'That's true.' Fleur didn't attempt to deny it. 'But there's something we have to talk about, and I think you know what it is.'

Helen's mouth dried. *No*, she thought unsteadily. *No*, she had nothing to say to this brittle woman, who she suspected was only here now because she was afraid of what Helen might tell the Sheridans. Through all the years she'd thought about her mother, and wondered what she was like, she'd never imagined confronting her like this. Dear God, she didn't even like her. It would have been so much simpler if they'd never ever met.

'I—don't think so,' she said at last, bending down to rescue one of Sophie's plastic sandals, which was in danger of being buried in the sand. Just go away, she begged silently. I really don't want to talk to you. I'll keep your dirty little secret, never fear.

'Please, Helen.' Fleur took off her dark glasses and gave her an appealing look. 'Don't you think I deserve a few minutes of your time? Is that really too much to ask?'

Helen took a breath. 'We've got nothing to say to one another,' she declared in a low voice, and Fleur sighed.

'Yes, we do,' she retorted. 'There may be some way I can help you. D'you think I like to see my—my daughter skivvying for someone else?'

Helen glanced anxiously towards Henry and Sophie, but to her relief they were still intent on destroying the castle. Henry appeared to have joined his sister now, in trampling down the battlements, and Helen wondered why she'd bothered to take so much trouble.

Without giving in to her mother's suggestion that they put some distance between themselves and the children, Helen compromised by turning her back on her charges. 'I don't need your help, thank you,' she said, without admitting their relationship. 'The Sheridans have been kind to me. Since—since Daddy died, I've learned who my real friends are.'

Fleur caught her lower lip between her teeth. 'I read—about what happened. I still have friends—acquaintances—in England, who thought it their responsibility to let me know that Jimmy had drowned. I would have got in touch with you then, but I was having—problems. Chase—Chase died a couple of months ago. I expect you knew that, too.'

'No. No, I didn't,' said Helen, not bothering to mention the fact that Matthew had told her. After all, what did it matter? She'd had no love for Chase Aitken.

'Well, he did.' Fleur visibly wilted. 'It was a terrible shock for—for all of us. He was such a young man.'

'My father was a young man, too.' Helen didn't attempt to sympathise with her. 'So—I suppose we've both lost a loved one. That's the only thing we've got in common.'

'No, it's not.' Fleur stretched out her hand, then, as Helen flinched away, she withdrew it again. 'Don't you want to know how I recognised you? It wasn't your name, Miss—*Graham*.'

Helen coloured. 'I didn't want you to recognise me,' she said, casting an unnecessary glance towards the children. 'I don't want you to recognise me now. It's been too many years; too many things have happened. I don't want to talk about it. I just wish you'd go away.'

Her mother sucked in her breath. 'You're very bitter.'

Helen stared at her. 'Wouldn't you be?'

'Perhaps.' Fleur had the grace to be honest. 'But, now that we've met again, can't we at least speak civilly to one another?'

'We are speaking civilly to one another.' Helen sighed. 'Look—just say what you have to say and go. Oh, and you needn't worry that I'll tell anyone about this meeting. Strange as it may seem, I've got some pride, too.'

Fleur bit her lip. 'You're just like me, you know.'

'No——'

'Yes.' Fleur hesitated. 'When I was your age, I looked a lot like you. Oh, you're taller, and you wear your hair longer, but that's not important. When I saw you at the party I was staggered no one else had seen the resemblance.'

Helen's lip curled. 'Is that supposed to be a compliment?'

Fleur laughed. 'Perhaps.' She lifted her shoulders. 'I see you've inherited Jimmy's arrogance. That's exactly how he'd have reacted if I'd said it to him.'

Helen bent her head. 'Is that all you wanted to say?'

'No.' Fleur regarded her with an expression that was hard to define. 'Believe it or not, I wanted to tell you my side of the story. I should never have married your father. Did he tell you that?'

'Frequently,' said Helen, though in truth James Gregory had never discussed his relationship with his wife. Like everything else about her mother, it had been banished. If he'd had any remorse, he'd never relayed it to her.

'Mmm.' Her mother absorbed what she'd said with a jaded smile, and Helen guessed she didn't believe a word. She had to remember that Fleur had known James Gregory rather well. And he simply hadn't been the type to expose his real feelings.

'Well,' Fleur said at last, 'you'll know, then, that our relationship was doomed from the start. Your father married me because he wanted children. I married him because I was a woman of passion. I needed a man's— attentions—to make me whole.'

Helen caught her breath. 'I don't want to hear this.'

'Why not?' Fleur seemed almost amused by her daughter's revulsion. 'It should reassure you. It should make you see that when I left I wasn't punishing you. I was punishing your father, I suppose, if that's relevant. You can't imagine what it was like. Our life was so dull!'

'Don't say any more.'

Helen tried to turn away, but Fleur continued relentlessly. 'Can't you even try to imagine how frustrated I was? All your father wanted was a brood mare. As soon as I'd had you, he began talking about how soon we could have another child, maybe a son this time. I stuck it for as long as I could, but when he found out I'd been using a contraceptive, he became impossible.'

'Please.'

Helen wanted to put her hands over her ears and run away, but with Henry and Sophie only yards from them there was little she could do.

'Listen to me,' Fleur persisted. 'Your father was a good man, but he was boring. I needed someone more—vital. Someone who wanted me, not just my genes.'

Helen gave her a tortured look. 'You found what you wanted with Chase Aitken, I suppose?' she said harshly, horrified to find she was on the verge of tears. 'Well, don't expect me to betray my father. He cared for me.

He cared for me deeply. You—you only cared for yourself.'

Fleur pulled a face. 'I knew you'd say that.'

'It's the truth.'

'Is it?' Fleur's lips twisted. 'I wonder. What if I told you I regretted marrying Chase, too? You see——' her small teeth tugged at her lower lip '—I think I married the wrong brother. But I'm hoping to get it right next time. Will you wish me luck?'

CHAPTER NINE

'WHAT?'

Lucas stared at him as if he couldn't believe his ears, and Matthew had to admit his statement had caused himself some astonishment, too. The only time he gave dinner parties was when his publisher or his agent came down from New York. He certainly didn't socialise with his neighbours, or invite them into his house.

'Well,' he said now, his tone revealing a defensiveness he would rather not have exposed, 'I've got to do something to get Fleur off my back. She's driving me crazy. God knows when I'll get this book finished.'

Lucas regarded him dourly. 'And how will giving a dinner party for the Sheridans get Fleur off your back?' he demanded. 'Dammit, you said you didn't even like them. Why invite them here?'

'Because it will give Fleur something to do—organising the menu, that sort of thing,' declared Matthew quickly. 'And as I've persuaded my father to leave the ranch for a couple of days, the least I can do is provide some entertainment.'

'Since when did Ben care about being entertained?' asked Lucas impatiently. 'And if you're doing this for me, then I'd sooner make my own arrangements, thank you.'

'For you——?' began Matthew blankly, and Lucas gave him an old-fashioned look.

'Yeah. So I can see Helen again,' he exclaimed, his expression becoming somewhat whimsical. 'If it's all the same to you, I'd as soon take her to the Greenhouse. The food there is excellent, and we won't have to worry about any of the Sheridans butting in.'

Matthew looked down at the pile of uncorrected manuscript on the desk in front of him, and mentally drew a breath. Anything to avoid looking into Lucas's open face. For God's sake, the idea that Lucas might misinterpret his motives that way hadn't even occurred to him. He was so wrapped up with his own selfish problems he hadn't given the other man a thought.

'Besides,' went on Lucas doggedly, 'I thought the last thing you'd want to do is appease the woman. Arranging parties for her is just playing into her hands. She'll get off both our backs much sooner if we ignore her. If there's one thing Fleur doesn't like it's to be bored.'

Matthew sighed. 'Maybe.'

'What do you mean, maybe? You know it's the truth. How long is she expecting to stay anyway? She's already been here over a week.'

Tell me about it, Matthew brooded to himself irritably, remembering the days before his sister-in-law's arrival with some nostalgia. Days before he'd met Helen, too, he acknowledged, before he could push the thought away. Which might prove even more significant, unless he could get her out of his head.

'I'm hoping that—given a little sweetener—she may decide to travel back to the ranch with my father,' he replied at last, though he doubted she'd go willingly. And was it fair to unload his problems on to the old man? he wondered grimly. Even with the financial settlement he had in mind, he sensed it wouldn't be that easy.

Lucas hunched his shoulders. 'Well, I think you're mad. And Ben will think so, too, when he gets here. You don't owe her a thing, Matt. She was your brother's wife, not yours. If he didn't make any sensible provision for her, why the hell should you?'

Because...

Because he'd once let Fleur think he was interested in her? Why else would she have come to his room that night, if not because he had been giving out the wrong signals? She'd believed he'd wanted her. Had she told

Chase about that? Was that why in recent years he'd seen so little of his brother? And, God forbid, was that the reason Chase had been drinking before he played that final—fatal—match?

'You're not—interested—in her, are you?'

Lucas had misinterpreted his silence, and his doubtful enquiry brought Matthew swiftly to his senses. 'God-dammit, no!'

Lucas breathed more easily. 'I'm glad to hear it. For a moment there, I wondered.'

Matthew's jaw tightened. It was impossible to discuss his original reasons for giving the party with Lucas now. For a while there, he'd forgotten how smitten with Helen his assistant was, and he felt ashamed when he considered what he'd been planning to do. In his experience, there was only one way to get a woman out of your system, and, while he'd known of the obvious dangers, he'd decided to take the risk.

But now...

'So you won't have any objections if I include Helen in the invitations?' Lucas went on, happily unaware of his employer's feelings, and Matthew gave a grudging shrug of his broad shoulders.

'Why should I?' he asked tautly, as if that wasn't exactly what he had been planning to do anyway. 'Though you may find the Sheridans won't appreciate the gesture.'

'Why not?' Lucas frowned. 'Oh—do you think they'll need her to babysit? I hadn't thought of that. You may be right.'

'I am right,' said Matthew equably, though until that moment he'd never even thought of it. He felt a growing swell of relief. 'Never mind, Luke. I'm asking the Longfords. They can bring Hazel along instead.'

Lucas gave him a dry look. 'Hazel Longford is a kid,' he said flatly. 'And I don't care to babysit myself.' He paused. 'Unless it's with Helen.' He looked suddenly thoughtful. 'I wonder how the Sheridans would feel about that?'

'Whatever the Sheridans would feel, I'd be bloody angry,' declared Matthew heavily. 'Forget it, Luke. I need you here.' Then, ignoring the mocking tug of his conscience, he added, 'If you want to see the woman, do it on your own time.'

The conversation ended soon after, and although Matthew had expected the other man to object to his heavy-handedness he hadn't. Lucas had probably put his attitude down to the continuing problem he was having with Fleur, he reflected. It was bloody hard not to feel guilty with so many paragons around.

An hour later, with the pile of manuscript hardly touched, Matthew had to concede that he was getting nowhere. His mind simply refused to concentrate on fiction, when his own life seemed to be running out of control.

With a feeling of raw impatience, he pushed his chair away from the desk. What was the matter with him? he thought irritably. Why couldn't he put the Graham woman's face out of his mind? And not just her face, he recalled unwillingly. He could still feel her small breasts against his chest . . .

He scowled at his watch. It was barely eleven o'clock. Far too early to think about meeting his father at the airport. Ben wasn't due to arrive until three-thirty. Even allowing for the time it would take to get there, he'd still got more than a couple of hours to fill.

Getting up from his chair, he walked broodingly over to the long windows. Beyond a flowering hedge, the still surface of the pool gleamed in silent invitation. But beside the pool, stretched out beneath a striped umbrella, Fleur was enjoying the brilliance of the day. Like the serpent in his particular Eden, she basked in the sun while he sweated in his study.

Matthew's scowl deepened. If Fleur hadn't been there, he would probably have taken a swim. A refreshing dip in cool water was exactly what he needed to clear his head. And cool his blood, he acknowledged tersely. It wasn't just the temperature that was making him hot.

But Fleur was there, and there was no way Matthew was going to join her. In his present state of mind, he might just say something he'd regret. Besides, he wasn't totally convinced that his body wouldn't betray him. And the last thing he wanted was for her to think she turned him on.

He swung away from the window and propped his hips against the broad sill. He ought to work, but doing so was no more inviting now than it had been minutes before. He needed to get out of the villa. He needed to put some space between his actions and his thoughts.

He'd go into Bridgetown, he decided abruptly. There was a book shop in Broad Street, and it was some weeks since he'd checked out the latest titles. Whenever he finished writing, he always enjoyed the relaxation he found in reading. It was such a relief to let some other author carry the story, and work out the final dénouement.

Lucas was working in the outer office, and he looked up in some surprise when his employer appeared. 'D'you want some coffee?' he asked. 'I can ask Ruth——'

'I don't want anything,' said Matthew firmly, realising that Lucas would think he was acting out of character. 'I—er—I thought I'd take a ride into town. I feel like having a break. I won't be long.'

'I'll come with you,' said Lucas at once, but Matthew pressed him back into his seat with a purposeful hand.

'No need,' he said, tempering his refusal with a grimace. 'I guess Fleur is getting me down. I need to cut me a little space, OK?'

'OK.'

But Lucas regarded him with doubtful eyes. What was he thinking? Matthew wondered ruefully as he strode along the cool marble tiles of the corridor. That he was seeking to assuage his conscience? That, however he denied it, he *was* attracted to his dead brother's widow?

A louvred door gave access to the rear of the villa. Here a pleasantly-shaded courtyard gave on to a range of outbuildings. This was the oldest part of the estate, with some of the buildings dating back to the eighteenth century. Unlike the house, which had been rebuilt from the foundations, what had once been the servants' quarters had been converted into a string of garages.

There were stables here, too, though Matthew didn't keep any horses. If he wanted to ride, there were hacks available, but, having been brought up with the cream of horseflesh, he was loath to accept anything less. Besides, when he visited the ranch—which wasn't often, he admitted ruefully—he spent most of his days on horseback. His father was a tireless rider, and he'd taught both his sons to appreciate the sport.

Too well? wondered Matthew wryly, adjusting his jean-clad thighs beneath the wheel of an open-topped buggy. He hoped his father wasn't blaming himself for Chase's death. His brother had always been mad on horses, right from being a schoolboy, and becoming a professional polo-player had seemed a natural progression.

The traffic into Bridgetown was fairly hectic, and, like every other tourist resort, the town was thronged with eager sightseers. Skins of every colour mingled in the busy shops along Broad Street, and Matthew thought he was incredibly lucky when he found a parking space just off the square.

Unlike some Caribbean resorts, however, Bridgetown had a distinctly British appeal. Many of the Gothic structures dated from the reign of Queen Victoria, and a monument to Lord Nelson stood impressively in Trafalgar Square.

Leaving the buggy, Matthew negotiated a narrow lane that led down into the main thoroughfare. To his left the inner basin of the Careenage provided a tranquil harbour for luxury yachts. It was a far cry from the busy port it had once been, its erstwhile warehouses converted now into pretty cafés and shops. To his right, St Michael's Row led along to the cathedral. One of the oldest surviving churches in Barbados, the cathedral had been rebuilt after its destruction in the hurricane of 1780.

Leaving the square, Matthew started along Broad Street. As well as shops, there were several office buildings here, their wrought-iron balconies giving the place a colonial feel.

Graftons, the book store he sought, was situated on the corner of Maize Street. Small and personal, it nevertheless stocked an enormous collection of reference books and novels, with guide books for the tourists and paperbacks for everyone.

The owner, Becky Grafton, was a grey-haired Barbadian, and she greeted Matthew with her usual cheerful smile. 'Morning, Mr Aitken,' she said. 'What can we do for you this morning?'

Matthew grinned. 'Nothing, thanks. I've come to browse.' He grimaced. 'Unfortunately, you don't stock inspiration, do you?'

'Depends what kind of inspiration you're looking for, man,' chuckled her assistant, Larry Kamada. 'I'm told folks get all kinds of ideas from some of the books we sell.'

Matthew was nodding good-humouredly when he glimpsed a familiar figure beyond the shelves. With his stomach tightening unwillingly, he felt sure it was Helen Graham. He'd have recognised that braid anywhere, and the slender elegance of her figure.

Fortunately someone came to pay for their books at that moment, and it enabled Matthew to excuse himself from Becky and her assistant. And, although common sense dictated that he leave his browsing until later, he ignored the warning voice and followed his senses.

He found her in the furthest corner of the shop, half hidden behind the final fixture. He was fairly certain she had seen him now, and was hoping to avoid him. But her pale limbs were too noticeable, particularly as she was only wearing a short denim skirt and a pink sleeveless vest.

'Good morning,' he said, forcing her to look up from the volume of poetry she was studying. 'Are you a fellow reader, Miss Graham?'

'It's——' she began, and then broke off, flushing. 'Um—yes. I enjoy reading. When I have the time.' She paused, and, having regained her composure, gave him a cool look. 'I haven't read any of your books, however.'

'It's not obligatory,' said Matthew, apparently unfazed, though the faint contempt in her voice wasn't welcome. 'What do you read, Miss Graham? Apart from——' he dipped his head '—my namesake, Matthew Arnold?'

Helen thrust the anthology back on to the shelf, and moved as if she would have gone past him. 'Lots of things,' she said. 'So long as they're interesting.' She took a short breath. 'Excuse me.'

'Novels?' Matthew knew it was crazy, but he wouldn't let her pass him. Not until he'd got her to relax with him at least. For God's sake, if Lucas had his way, she'd be invited to Dragon Bay. They couldn't meet with animosity between them.

'Occasionally,' she acknowledged now, and he knew she was only answering him to avoid an argument. But, hell, when he was with her, he couldn't help being aware of her. For some reason, she disturbed him in a wholly unfamiliar way.

'You're alone?' he persisted, wondering where her charges were this morning, and he could fairly feel the antagonism surging through her.

'For the moment,' she said tightly. Then, 'Will you please move out of my way? I've some other errands I want to run and you're making me late.'

Matthew took a deep breath, and folded his arms across his chest. He looked relaxed, he thought, but his fingers were digging into the dark blue silk of his sleeve. He'd rolled the sleeves back to his elbows, and the muscles in his forearms tightened reflexively. But he'd never get another chance like this, and he wasn't about to lose it.

'What do you mean?' he said at last. 'You said, "for the moment". Do I take it the little horrors are with you? Or have you left them back at the house?'

Her tongue appeared and circled her lips. It was a pink tongue, Matthew noticed, and there was something unknowingly sensual in the way she moistened her lips. Not that she was aware of it. He'd gamble on that assumption. She was simply weighing the odds of lying to him or simply telling the truth.

The truth apparently won out. 'If you mean my charges,' she replied stiffly, 'they're spending the day with their parents. Tricia and Drew—Mr and Mrs Sheridan, that is—are visiting some friends in Speightstown. And, as their friends have got children, they've taken Henry and Sophie with them.'

'Really?' Matthew felt an unwarranted surge of exhilaration. He felt as if someone had just handed him a present, but one which he wasn't supposed to accept.

'Yes, really,' Helen repeated shortly, clearly eager to be on her way. 'Now, will you let me pass? Or must I call the assistant? As you're apparently known here, I don't suppose you'd like it if I screamed.'

Matthew's lips compressed. 'So you did see me come in,' he remarked, ignoring the implied threat. 'Was that why you panicked and hid in this corner?'

'I did not panic.' But her nervous lips betrayed her. 'I simply didn't want to speak to you, that's all.'

'Why not?'

'Why not?' She regarded him with frustrated eyes. 'I should have thought that was obvious, in the circumstances.' Then, as if gathering some courage from his silence, 'For a writer, you're extremely unimaginative. If you give it some thought, I'm sure you'll understand.'

Once again, she attempted to go past him, but this time she came up against the unyielding wall of his body. If she'd thought that by insulting him she'd cause him to lose interest, he reflected, then she didn't know him very well at all.

'It's a little late to play hard to get, isn't it?' he asked, as she recoiled from the heat of his chest. 'Just because I didn't finish what I started, don't pretend you spent the whole time fighting me off.'

Her colour deepened then, and in spite of himself Matthew was intrigued. She was such a curious mixture of sensuality and innocence, and although he didn't believe the latter, he wanted to prolong this encounter.

It took her a minute to compose herself again, and then she said in a low voice, 'If you've finished, I'd like to go. Please.'

Matthew frowned. 'And if I'm not?'

'Not what?'

She was confused now. He could tell by the blank look in her eyes that his earlier accusation had found its mark. But, contrarily, it didn't please him. Her submission was no more appealing than her retaliation had been.

'Not finished,' he said almost gently, and, acting purely on instinct, he stepped aside. 'Look, can we just forget what happened last week? Let's put it down to experience. Why don't you let me buy you lunch, to prove there's no hard feelings?'

'I can't.'

Her immediate denial annoyed him, but at least she hadn't rushed away. 'Why can't you?' he asked evenly. 'There's a café just round the corner.'

'I've got to get back,' she said automatically, but he sensed that she was weakening. 'Mr Aitken, there's no need for you to do this. We'll say no more about it.'

Matthew sighed, controlling his impatience with an effort. 'You said yourself that the Sheridans are away all day,' he reminded her.

'I know.'

'So there's really no reason for you to hurry back?'

'Perhaps not.'

He took a gamble. 'But you find my company objectionable? You'd rather eat alone.' He shrugged. 'Well, OK, if that's the way you feel, there's nothing more to say.'

'No.'

She did move then, tucking the strap of her bag over her shoulder and starting towards the door. Matthew was just consoling himself with the thought that she'd probably done him a favour, however unlikely that felt at the moment, when she glanced back over her shoulder and stopped.

'Just around the corner?' she said, coming back on what were obviously reluctant feet. 'The café? That is what you said, isn't it?'

Matthew's stomach contracted. 'Yeah.' He paused. 'Down on the quay, if you know where that is.'

'I do.' She hesitated. Then, 'Why not?' She shrugged. 'If you really meant it, that is. If you weren't just being—polite.'

All the air seemed to go out of Matthew's lungs, and all he could do was nod. And, with a gesture of compliance, Helen turned again and sauntered towards the exit. He knew she couldn't be feeling as nonchalant as she appeared from behind, that if he looked into her eyes he'd see the uncertainty that still lingered, but he had to admire her confidence all the same.

He watched her as she traversed the aisle ahead of him, and he was aware of the possession in his gaze. But hell, the tail of that neat braid, bobbing about at her waist, was absurdly sexy, her slim legs long and curvaceous below the short hem of her skirt. He wouldn't have been human, he told himself, if he hadn't remembered how she'd looked that evening nearly a week ago. He'd wanted to make love with her then, and he wanted to now.

There was a half-moon of sunburned skin above the scooped neckline of her vest, and as he came up behind her at the entrance he knew the craziest urge to bend and soothe it with his tongue. But then his eyes encountered Larry Kamada's and he quickly stifled the impulse. He was letting his senses rule his reason, and it had to stop.

The café he took her to overlooked the Careenage, and for a while, as the waiter took their order and Helen's attention was diverted by the gleaming yachts lying at anchor, Matthew was able to convince himself that he'd imagined the way he'd felt. She was attractive and sexy,

and—hell!—she probably knew it better than he did.
That diffidence was just an act; he was sure of it.

They sat outside, at a table shaded by a huge umbrella. With the sun dazzling on the water, and the sound
of muted conversation all around them, it was all very
normal and civilised. Matthew decided that anyone
watching them would assume they were holidaying
together.

Or perhaps not, he considered. His arms and legs were
tanned while Helen's skin was still fashionably pale. Like
the back of her neck, where the sun had caught her, her
skin turned pink. An indication of its delicacy that he
was loath to admit he'd noticed.

They ate shellfish and salad—juicy island shrimp
served with mixed greens and papaya. There were spicy
sauces to accompany the food, and Matthew noticed
Helen avoided them. But she did drink several glasses
of the dry Californian wine he'd ordered, and he guessed
that she was thirsty.

'Nice?' he ventured, after their plates had been taken
away, and because the wine had relaxed her Helen
nodded.

'Very nice,' she conceded, elbows lodged on the table,
her wine-glass cradled between her palms. 'Thank you,'
she added belatedly. 'It was kind of you to bring me
here. My—my father and I used to come to Barbados
many moons ago.'

Matthew hesitated. 'But your father's dead now,' he
averred softly, and she gave him a guarded look.

'How do you know that?'

Matthew sighed. 'Oh—Luke told me, I think.' He
hoped he hadn't spoiled the mood. 'It's not a secret, is
it?'

'A secret?' Her lips twisted suddenly, but, although
he'd been half-afraid he'd said the wrong thing, she
shook her head. 'No, that's not a secret. He—died seven
months ago.'

'I'm sorry.'

'Yes.' She grimaced. 'So am I.' Then, with a sudden change of direction, 'How long were Fleur and your brother married?'

Matthew didn't want to talk about Fleur at this point, but he humoured her. 'Oh—about seventeen years, I guess,' he said carelessly. 'I was sixteen when Chase brought her to live with us. They weren't married then, of course. Fleur's husband hadn't divorced her.'

Helen put down her glass. 'She was already married, then, when your brother found her?'

'What is this?' Matthew was impatient, and it showed. But, dammit, why was she interested in Fleur? It wasn't as if the two women even liked one another.

'What do you mean?' A faint trace of colour had entered her cheeks again, and Matthew wondered how it was that he could disconcert her so easily. And then he thought he had the solution. She was talking about Fleur to prevent him from saying anything provocative.

Shaking his head, he said, 'OK. She was married, right? But if you're implying that Chase broke up a happy marriage, you couldn't be more wrong. There'd been men before him, I'm convinced of it. If you knew Fleur as well as I do, you'd know she's one hungry lady!'

Helen's colour dissolved as quickly as it had appeared. In seconds her face was completely white, and Matthew knew an unfamiliar sense of concern. He guessed the combination of the heat, the dazzling sun and an unaccustomed amount of wine was responsible for her pallor. She needed somewhere cool and shady, where she could relax for a while.

'Are you all right?' he asked, and she looked at him with unexpectedly wounded eyes.

'I'm fine,' she said quickly, though she clearly wasn't. 'Um—thank you for lunch. I've got to go——'

'Not yet,' said Matthew firmly, grasping her wrist when she would have risen from the table. 'Let me get the bill, and then I'll see you back to the villa.'

'No—I—I've brought Maria's car,' she protested, but Matthew knew she was in no condition to drive.

'I guess they have laws about drinking and driving here, too,' he informed her softly. 'Now, just sit still a minute. You're in no fit state to go anywhere alone.'

'Wine doesn't make me drunk,' she exclaimed faintly, after Matthew had summoned the waiter and arranged to pay. 'Please, let me go. Everyone's looking.'

'Only because you're making a scene,' Matthew informed her drily. 'Take it easy, can't you? We'll be out of here directly, I promise.'

He noticed, with some relief, that her colour was returning as they left the table. But he retained his hold on her arm, just in case she felt a little weak. Besides, although he didn't want to admit it, he enjoyed looking after her. He liked the feeling of her fine bones beneath his hand, though he sensed her resistance was only dormant and not totally suppressed.

At the corner of Broad Street she halted. 'I think this is where we part company,' she said, obliging him to release her. 'Thank you again for lunch. It was most—unexpected.'

Matthew drew a breath. 'You're going to drive back?'

Her brows arched. 'Of course.'

'Then, where are you parked? I'll follow you. Just to make sure you're all right.'

Helen's mouth tightened. 'There's no need.'

'I think there is.'

'Why?' She gazed at him angrily. 'Aren't there any *hungry* ladies for you to annoy around here?'

Matthew's lips parted. 'Did that upset you?' he exclaimed. 'Was that why you looked so sick back at the restaurant?' He shook his head. 'Hey, I've never satisfied Fleur's particular appetite. If you think I was speaking from experience, you were wrong.'

'It's of supreme indifference to me,' she declared, turning away. 'Goodbye, Mr Aitken. I don't suppose I'll see you again.'

The hell you won't, Matthew muttered to himself irritably. For God's sake, what was wrong with what he'd said? Fleur was nothing to her; they hardly knew one another. Yet there was no denying she'd reacted to his words.

He gnawed broodingly at his lower lip as he walked back to where he had left the buggy. It wasn't until he was on his way home that he remembered he hadn't bought the books he'd intended to buy. Meeting Helen had put everything else out of his head, he thought frustratedly. And for all she'd had lunch with him, he was fairly sure she still resented him like hell.

And why? Because he'd come on to her one time? Well, maybe more than come on to her, he admitted honestly, but it wasn't as if she'd been wholly opposed to what he'd done. If he hadn't come to his senses as he had, he had the feeling she wouldn't have stopped him. Was that what was eating her? Was she blaming him for being a tease?

If she only knew, he reflected bitterly, feeling the tight constriction of his trousers. What he really wanted was for them to spend the afternoon in bed. Then maybe both of them could get it out of their systems. There was no denying his frustration as he drove back to Dragon Bay.

CHAPTER TEN

'WHERE did you go today?' Tricia asked at supper, and Helen wished she'd had more warning of the question. She'd foolishly assumed that the Sheridans would think she'd spent the day at the villa. But evidently Maria had been talking, and there was no escape.

'I went into Bridgetown this morning,' she replied, aware of Andrew's eyes upon her. But then they'd been on her since she had joined them at the table, and she wished she'd worn something less revealing.

But it was so hot tonight, and the ankle-length skirt and chiffon blouse had looked perfectly adequate in her bedroom. It was only now that she was aware of the blouse's transparency, and the fact that the skirt was slit to the knee.

'Yes. Maria said you'd taken her car,' Tricia remarked, with some impatience. 'I'd have thought you'd have welcomed some time alone instead of rubbing shoulders with a crowd of tourists.'

'We're tourists,' put in Andrew mildly, but Tricia was obviously in no mood to accommodate her husband.

'Not that kind of tourists,' she said. 'We're sort of staying with friends. In any case, I thought Helen might be tired.'

'She's not an old woman,' Andrew inserted, and earned a malevolent look from his wife.

'Like me, you mean?' she countered. 'I know that's what you were really saying. You embarrassed me at the Rutherfords as well.'

Andrew gave a resigned sigh. 'I did not embarrass you,' he retorted. 'But if you must go around telling everyone what a saint you are, you must expect a little fire and brimstone in response.'

Tricia's eyes flashed. 'I did not tell everyone I was a saint——'

'As good as,' countered Andrew laconically. 'And I doubt Helen would approve of her affairs being gossiped about indiscriminately. You had no right to tell them about her father. Or her mother either, as it happens. It's nothing to do with——'

'What have you been saying about my mother?' Helen, who had been congratulating herself on avoiding any mention of Matthew Aitken, now felt a sudden twinge of alarm. 'What do you know about my mother?' she protested anxiously. 'I—I've never even mentioned her to you.'

'I haven't said anything,' denied Tricia irritably, though the glance she cast in her husband's direction promised retribution later. 'I simply told them you were my nanny, and someone—I don't remember who—asked if you were James Gregory's daughter. Of course I had to say you were, and that was that.'

'But what did they say about—about him?' she finished lamely, realising she couldn't mention Fleur's name without creating more confusion, and Tricia sighed.

'Nothing that you haven't told me yourself,' she replied impatiently. 'Drew's exaggerating, as usual. For goodness' sake, it's not a secret, is it? It was in the papers when it happened.'

'What Trish means is that people are naturally curious,' Andrew declared now, evidently deciding the joke had gone far enough. 'If she hadn't made such a big thing out of employing someone without any previous experience, I doubt your name would have come into it. But as she compared her actions to those of Mother Teresa——'

'That is not true!'

Tricia was incensed, but Helen didn't find their bickering amusing any more.

'Well, you were waxing lyrical about how generous you'd been to Helen,' Andrew persisted unrepentantly.

'For heaven's sake, after spending a day in the offspring's company, I'd say she deserved a medal, not you.'

'They're your children,' retorted Tricia, but her eyes flickered somewhat remorsefully in the younger woman's direction. 'Oh—what does it matter anyway?' she exclaimed with feeling. 'Nobody knows you here.'

Except Fleur, thought Helen uneasily. And how would she react if these friends—whoever they were—knew Matthew, and mentioned it to him? So far, he only knew her as Helen Graham. But even he might make the connection if he was pushed.

At least her own activities weren't questioned any further. So far as the Sheridans were concerned she had spent the morning in Bridgetown, and that was that. Besides, Matthew Aitken had been the last person she'd expected to meet in a bookshop. Although, now she came to think of it, it wasn't as unlikely as all that.

In any event, they'd never suspect that he might have bought her lunch. Encountering him was one thing; having him spend time—and money—on her was another. She didn't even know why he'd done it. He certainly didn't know that Fleur was her mother.

Which was, of course, why she had accepted his invitation. Without the fact that she'd wanted to question him about his brother's relationship with Fleur, she'd never have spent any longer with him than she had to. As it was, she'd found out rather more than she'd expected, and, although she'd told herself that she didn't believe everything he'd said, she couldn't forget what her mother had said about marrying the wrong brother.

The next few days passed reasonably uneventfully. Now that Andrew was here the Sheridans went out occasionally in the evening, either to friends' houses or to dine at one of the better restaurants in the area. Thankfully Helen wasn't expected to accompany them, and she spent most of her evenings reading, or listening to the World Service, which she could tune in to on Maria's radio.

Henry and Sophie had settled down to a regular routine, and to Helen's relief her mother didn't try to contact her again. Whether she would, when Helen was back in London, was another matter. For all she told herself she didn't want to see Fleur again, the memories still hurt.

Then, towards the end of their second week, an invitation arrived. It was from Dragon Bay, from Matthew Aitken, and Tricia couldn't wait to tell Helen that she'd been right.

'I knew he'd invite us to his house,' she declared. 'It would have been terribly rude if he hadn't. Apparently his father is staying with them, and he'd like us to join them for lunch tomorrow.'

'Lunch?' echoed Helen in surprise, and Tricia bridled.

'Yes. He says we should bring the children along as well.' She grimaced. 'I bet that was his assistant's idea. What was his name? Lucas? I noticed his interest in you, and I suppose it's the only way he could get you to come, too.'

'Me?' echoed Helen, aghast, and Tricia nodded.

'Yes, you,' she exclaimed shortly. 'I forgot to mention it. Your name's on the invitation as well.'

Helen spent the next twenty-four hours wondering how she could get out of going. She didn't want to see Matthew's house, and she was fairly sure her mother wouldn't want her there either. Whatever Matthew had said, Fleur evidently thought she had some hope of achieving her ambitions. Helen didn't want to watch her trying. She just wanted to get on with her life.

Besides, she thought unhappily, she didn't want to have to explain to Tricia and Andrew why she hadn't mentioned meeting Matthew in Bridgetown. And as for admitting they had had lunch...

It was all getting horribly complicated, and it was all Matthew Aitken's fault. Why did he have to play his games with her? Wasn't one member of her family good enough for him?

Of course, he didn't know who Fleur was, and she had no intention of telling him. The opinions he'd voiced about her mother were hardly flattering. The last thing she wanted was for him to think that she was like that, too.

And yet, who could blame him if he had misinterpreted her actions? But, until that incident on the beach, she'd never imagined she could lose control. Perhaps due to her father's unhappy experience, she had kept her relationships with men strictly casual. She'd reached the ripe old age of twenty-two without ever giving her heart—or herself—to anyone.

Unwillingly, the memory of how she'd felt when Matthew cornered her in the bookshop came back to haunt her. She hadn't believed it when she'd heard his voice, and she'd taken cover almost instinctively. But he'd seen her. His sharp gaze had located her, hidden behind the bookshelves. She'd snatched up that anthology of Matthew Arnold just seconds before he'd appeared.

She wondered if it was fate that had caused her to choose *Matthew* Arnold. Goodness knew, there had been any number of other writers she could have picked. But her hand had reached unerringly for the nineteenth-century poet, although she couldn't remember a word she'd read.

She sighed. It had amused Matthew. Accusing her of panicking, forcing her practically to beg him to get out of her way. And watching her with those cool green eyes, enjoying her disconcertment. She'd been afraid he was going to touch her, but he'd been far too clever for that.

Her mouth felt dry just remembering how he'd made her feel. Her breasts had suddenly felt absurdly tender, and there'd been a disturbing pain low in her stomach. She'd felt hot, too, hot and sticky, especially between her legs. She'd been so afraid he'd notice; so afraid he'd do something to embarrass her all over again.

And, despite her protestations, panic had won out. She had tried to get past him, tried to force her way to the door through the immovable wall of his chest. She hadn't succeeded; not until he'd let her. All she'd gained was a trembling awareness of the sensual heat of his body.

She hardly remembered what they'd said. She knew he'd made some comment about her choice of reading material, and she'd retaliated by putting him down. But she hadn't read any of his books, she defended herself fiercely. And his head was quite big enough without her adding to his ego.

Of course, he had derided her resistance to his teasing. And if she'd had any sense, she'd have made her escape as soon as he let her go. But, instead of that, she'd agreed to have lunch with him. And however honourable her motives had been, she'd been aware of him every second they were together.

Yet, she sighed inwardly, it hadn't been all bad. When Matthew wasn't baiting her or asking awkward questions, he could be really nice. And the food had been delicious, the surroundings equally as good. With the yachts rocking at anchor, and the sun dancing on the water, it had been absolutely heaven—until she'd asked about Fleur...

Did she believe him? That was the point. Did she want to believe him, and was she in danger of condemning her own mother on the strength of what Matthew had said? And, finally, was she any better? Had she just not had the opportunity to expose her own unstable nature?

By the following morning she had resigned herself to the fact that she had to go. For her own peace of mind, if nothing else. She had to prove to herself, once and for all, that Matthew Aitken meant nothing to her. That the animosity she'd felt towards her mother was not simply—jealousy.

'Are you going like that?' Tricia exclaimed disparagingly, when she appeared on the terrace in her usual attire of T-shirt and shorts. 'You are going for lunch, Helen. Don't you think a dress—or even a skirt—would be more suitable?'

'Well, I think Helen looks very nice as she is,' remarked Andrew, with predictable arrogance. 'You should wear shorts, Trish. Then your legs wouldn't look so deathly white. Helen's acquiring quite a tan, even though her skin's as fair as yours.'

'Helen isn't a redhead,' retorted Tricia, stung, as usual, by her husband's ability to put her down. 'And I think wearing shorts is *passé*, especially on a formal occasion. Though I suppose Helen will be eating with the children...' She paused. 'Perhaps she has a point.'

Helen didn't choose to comment. Between them they'd succeeded in making her feel like the poor relation, but perhaps that was to her advantage. And she was poor, if not an actual relation. And it would suit her very well if she had only Henry and Sophie to deal with.

'Will we see the dragons?' asked Sophie, after she and her brother and Helen had been installed in the back of the estate car, and her mother gave an exasperated sigh.

'How many more times?' she exclaimed. 'Sophie, there are no dragons. It's just the name of a house, that's all. Now, please, sit down and shut up.'

It took about fifteen minutes to reach Matthew's house by road. Helen had half expected they'd go via the beach, as Matthew and the others had done the evening they'd dined with the Sheridans. But Tricia had insisted that she couldn't walk so far in the blazing sun. It was different after dark, she'd added. It was cooler, and one didn't perspire quite so much.

Which was true, Helen reflected, if one had a car with air-conditioning. The Parrishs' estate car had no such refinements, and the heat in the back was almost unbearable. Tricia had insisted that Andrew couldn't possibly have all the windows open or her hair would lose its style. And, as she'd spent most of the morning getting ready, Helen wasn't really surprised.

Nevertheless, by the time they reached the private road leading to Dragon Bay Sophie was feeling sick, and Helen's nerves were stretched as tight as violin-strings. She assured herself it was the child's health that was troubling her, and not the thought of their destination, but she wasn't convinced. Still, if Sophie was ill, perhaps she and the children could go home. She doubted Tricia would object. She hadn't wanted them here in the first place.

Stone gateposts marked the entrance to Matthew's property, and they crunched down a coral shale drive, between hedges of flowering hibiscus. The perfume of the flowers invaded the car, filling the air with a heady fragrance.

Further on, acres of manicured lawns came into view, their lushness enhanced by the continual use of sprinklers. They could see the house now, too, a sprawling two-storey dwelling, and Tricia exclaimed excitedly, delighted she'd got her way.

But it was an attractive house, even Helen had to concede that. Peach-coloured brick, weathered to a creamy radiance, was topped by a pink-tiled roof, whose eaves drooped protectively over wrought-iron balconies. A profusion of pink and white bougainvillaea trailed delightfully over the walls, and many long windows were trimmed with shutters.

'What a place!' breathed Tricia, nudging her husband's arm, as they reached a tree-shaded courtyard. A stone nymph holding a pitcher tipped water tirelessly into a basin, creating an illusion of coolness in its lily-strewn depths. 'All this, and the ocean, too,' she added enviously, nodding towards the turquoise water just visible beyond the adobe wall that enclosed the stables. 'Imagine living here in such luxury! No wonder Fleur wants to hang on to her connection with the family.'

Her words disturbed Helen, but Sophie chose that moment to wail, 'I'm going to be sick!' and Helen tumbled her out of the car before it happened. In consequence, she was attending to the little girl when Matthew appeared around the side of the house, and she wondered if she was ever destined to meet this man on equal terms.

But, before Matthew could speak to her, Tricia thrust open her door and intercepted him. 'I'm so sorry,' she said, by way of a greeting. 'I'm afraid my daughter is a proper pain. She doesn't seem able to travel a hundred yards without having this problem. It was kind of you to invite the children, but perhaps you shouldn't have bothered.'

'Nonsense.' Matthew, in a black silk shirt, open down his chest to display the smooth brown skin of his torso, gave Tricia's apologies short shrift. He ran a careless hand over the light covering of dark hair that thickened around his navel, and despite herself Helen's eyes were drawn to the way it arrowed beneath his belt. Tight black jeans, worn to a comfortable softness, moulded his powerful thighs, and she had to tear her gaze from the muscles that bulged against his zip. 'I can remember not being a particularly good traveller myself at Sophie's age. Especially in hot weather,' he appended drily, and Helen was sure he'd noticed that all the car windows were shut.

'Beautiful place you've got here, old man,' Andrew remarked, evidently deciding not to make an issue of the children. 'What is it? An acre or so?'

'Two acres of gardens, and a further half-dozen that are uncultivated,' replied Matthew shortly. He glanced at Helen again, who was drying Sophie's face with a tissue now. 'Come along. I'll introduce you to my father. Then I'll show Helen where she can wash Sophie's face.'

'Oh, I'm sure that's not——' began Tricia protestingly, but Henry disconcerted her by running up to Matthew and grabbing his hand.

'Are there really no dragons?' he asked, proving he was not as sophisticated as he'd pretended, and Sophie pursed her lips because he'd stolen her thunder.

'Only little ones,' Matthew replied good-humouredly, pointing out one of the tiny lizards that clung to the trunk of a tree. 'Of the animal variety, anyway,' he added, with another glance at Helen. 'But we do have some monkeys as neighbours, and you might see one of them if you're lucky.'

'I hope you're not referring to us, old man,' exclaimed Andrew, laughing, but Tricia didn't find that amusing at all.

'It's so hot,' she said affectedly. 'I'm looking forward to a cool martini. Oh—look, what a delightful pool! It's not like that poky one back at the villa, where you can't even get a decent swim.'

As Tricia hadn't even wet her toes in the pool at the villa, Helen couldn't quite see her argument, but it was true that the huge swimming-pool, nestling among flowering cannas and ginger lilies, was spectacular. A row of cabanas provided a colourful side-screen, with striped chairs and loungers set beneath tall umbrellas. Above the cabanas an arched bell-tower added a touch of character, and gave an indication of the Mediterranean style of the villa.

The back of the building, which faced the sea, was built on three sides of a paved courtyard. A cloister-like veranda, threaded with flowering vines, jutted out at the first-floor level. Above this there were balconies, shadowed, as before, by the hanging eaves. Helen guessed all the rooms inside the house would be cool and shaded. Whoever had designed the building had had its occupants' comfort in mind.

In the centre of the courtyard, matching the one at the other side of the house, a fountain played incessantly. And it was around the fountain that a selection of chairs and tables had been arranged, carefully protected by a shady canopy.

Fleur, dressed more modestly today in a simple apricot sheath, was seated beside an older man with greying dark hair. Matthew's father, obviously, Helen decided, hanging on to Sophie's sticky hand. He got to his feet as they stepped into the courtyard, and his warm smile was disturbingly like his son's.

Matthew made the introductions while Fleur looked on, and Helen saw—to her relief, she told herself—that her mother had no intention of betraying their relationship. The smile she cast in her daughter's direction was no more and no less condescending than the smile she offered their other guests. She didn't even get to her feet to greet them. She simply proffered a languid hand.

'Sophie's been sick,' Matthew announced, after acquainting his father with the names of their guests. 'I'm just going to show Helen to a bathroom where she can clean the little girl up. Dad, can I leave you to give these people a drink? I know Tricia would like a martini.'

'No problem,' said Ben Aitken easily, giving Helen a knowing look. 'Don't worry about us. We can look after ourselves. Show her the house, why don't you?'

The look Matthew exchanged with his father was no less exasperated than the look Fleur cast at her daughter. 'Surely—Helen—can manage on her own,' she said. 'There's a bathroom off the gallery. You don't need to escort her, Matt. She's not a child as well.'

'But I want to,' replied Matthew smoothly, causing Helen no small twinge of anxiety, and she felt like assuring all of them that she was here against her will. Only Sophie seemed delighted at the unexpected attention, and, trying to remember the child's feelings, she followed Matthew into the house.

Her impressions, such as they were, were of cool marble tiles and tall, pale walls. A shallow staircase wound against one wall, flanked by a banister made of some dark wood that had been polished to a mirror-bright sheen. Then darkly-polished floors, strewn with thick Chinese carpets, and cool air from a system that controlled the atmosphere.

There were pictures on the walls lining the staircase, set at intervals between long windows. There were carved occasional tables that supported bowls of flowers, and urns of some stemmed foliage that gave off a fragrant scent.

They passed several pairs of double doors before Matthew halted before those at the end of the long corridor. Taking a handle in each hand, he threw the doors open, and indicated that Helen and Sophie should precede him inside.

Despite her determination not to be impressed by him or his house, Helen couldn't quite stifle the gasp that escaped her as she viewed what she could only assume was a guest suite. A sitting-room, elegantly furnished in olive leather and pale oak, gave access to the bedroom beyond. Through a wide archway, Helen glimpsed an enormous square divan, spread with turquoise silk. Long curtains, whose colour matched the bedspread, moved gently in the controlled air, allowing a view of the balcony, with the sun-kissed ocean as a backdrop.

Helen would have liked to stand and stare some more, but Matthew was already heading across the sitting-room to another door. 'It's in here,' he said. And, at her momentarily dazed look, 'The bathroom. I'll come back in a few minutes to take you downstairs.'

'Oh—oh, yes.'

Helen blinked her eyes and, tightening her grip on Sophie's hand, hurried across the thick Chinese rug that lay like a magic carpet in the middle of the polished floor. He probably thought she was stupid, she thought, acting like a schoolgirl in a sweet shop. But even the places she'd stayed with her father hadn't prepared her for this, and, like Sophie, she was silenced by her surroundings.

'Just use what you like,' he said as she stepped into a pale green cave, whose walls were finely veined marble tiles, inset with mirrors. Their reflections were diffused into a thousand different images, and Helen felt her colour deepen as she saw the way her clothes were clinging to her.

But it had been so hot in the car, and the scoop-necked T-shirt she'd worn over her swimsuit was already pasted to her back. Her shorts clung, too, delineating the cleft of her bottom, and crumpling up between her legs to expose her upper thighs.

But it was the way her breasts were outlined against the front of the T-shirt that caused her the most embarrassment. The reaction she had to Matthew Aitken was evident in every thrusting line. Despite her swimsuit, and the cotton shirt, her nipples pressed against the cloth, and she had no doubt that he'd noticed it as well.

Taking a trembling breath, she turned to close the door and found him gone. While she had been steeling herself to meet his mocking gaze, Matthew had left the suite. There was no one in the sitting-room, no one in the bedroom, as far as she could see. Just herself and Sophie, and these very beautiful rooms.

CHAPTER ELEVEN

'WHAT'S this?'

Unaware, Helen had released Sophie's hand, and now the little girl was poking her finger into a bowl of dried flowers standing at one end of the vanitory unit.

'Oh—um—pot-pourri,' Helen said absently, still glancing over her shoulder. And then, trying to regain her confidence, 'It's scented, sweetheart. Leave it alone.'

The bathroom was huge, with an enormous whirlpool bath and a shower cubicle besides. A bank of soft cream towels resided on a rack beside the twin basins, and a glass shelf displayed an assortment of bath-oils, gel and other preparations.

Helen noticed all the preparations were of a masculine variety. And, as she ventured to peep inside the glass cupboards, she found shaving-soap and razors, and deodorants for men. It couldn't be, she thought; he wouldn't allow them to use *his* bathroom. Yet, unless the room was Lucas's, who else's could it be?

Deciding she had spent quite enough time speculating about unessentials, Helen plucked Sophie's questing finger out of a jar of shower gel and handed her a tablet of soap instead. Then, turning on the gold taps, she filled one of the basins and, using a facecloth from the pile, she quickly washed the little girl's face.

'Mmm, this soap smells lovely,' said Sophie, enjoying herself immensely, and Helen's hopes of leaving the party early died a death. The child was always like this—down one minute and up the next. Once she was out of the car, she soon recovered her spirits.

'Well, hurry up and wash your hands,' said Helen a little tersely, realising she was blaming Sophie for something that was all her fault really. But, heavens, the idea

141

that this was Matthew's bathroom, that he had stood naked before these mirrors, excited her in ways she didn't comprehend. She only knew that it wasn't wise for her to be here. She was far too vulnerable at the moment.

The sound of the outer door opening gave her a start, but the woman who appeared presented no problem. She was small and round and maternal, and Helen guessed she must be in her fifties. With salt-and-pepper hair and button-black eyes, she had a smile that split her swarthy features.

'You all finished?' she asked, and Helen wondered if she'd come to clear up after them. She'd tidied the basin as best she could, but it was no longer in its previously pristine condition. And Sophie's fingermarks were probably everywhere. The little girl had an inquisitive nature.

But, 'Yes,' she said now, managing a rueful smile. 'Thanks very much.'

'It's no trouble.' The woman's accent was faintly middle-European. 'Come.' She held out her hand to Sophie. 'We will see if we can find some lemonade. And perhaps some ice-cream, hmm?'

Sophie looked up at Helen. 'Can I?'

'I don't see why not,' agreed Helen, patting her shoulder. 'You go along with Mrs——'

'It's Ruth,' said the woman. 'Just Ruth.' She took Sophie's hand in hers and smiled confidingly. 'Your brother will be envious, eh? Only little girls who've been unwell are offered my ice-cream.'

'And it's delicious,' declared Matthew, appearing behind her, and Ruth looked up at her employer with teasing eyes.

'How would you know?' she asked. 'You're not a little girl, are you?' She glanced down at Sophie again. 'He's just trying to butter me up.'

'What does that mean?' asked Sophie, as Ruth urged her past her employer and into the corridor beyond. 'Do you use butter to...?'

The child's voice grew indistinct, and, realising she hadn't moved since Matthew appeared, Helen quickly gathered herself together. 'She—she's very good—your housekeeper?' she finished questioningly. And, at his nod, 'Thanks again. I was feeling rather—sticky.'

Matthew inclined his head, but he didn't move out of the doorway, and, realising she couldn't hear Sophie any more, Helen took an uneasy breath. 'I'd better go,' she said. 'And—and join the others. Tricia will be wondering where I am. Henry can be such a handful.'

'But he is *her* handful,' Matthew pointed out, without budging, and Helen shook her head.

'I'm—I'm supposed to look after both children,' she said. 'That's why the Sheridans employ me. And if I know Tricia, she'll already be annoyed that I've seen your house and she hasn't.'

'But you haven't seen my house,' pointed out Matthew evenly. 'Only the hall and stairs, and these apartments. There are five other suites, sitting-rooms, dining-rooms and a couple of offices. Not to mention a library, my study and the kitchen.'

Helen expelled a nervous breath. 'Very impressive.'

'It wasn't said to impress. I was only stating what there was to see.' He glanced around. 'These are my apartments. Would you like to see the view from the balcony? It encompasses the whole of Dragon Bay.'

'Oh—well, I——' Helen licked her dry lips. Once again she had been put in the position of indebtedness to him, and to refuse what, on the face of it, was a simple request seemed rather churlish. 'Why not?'

'Good.'

He smiled, an unguarded smile this time, but she noticed he closed the doors behind him before advancing across the floor. They were shut into these rooms now, alone in his apartments. She wouldn't have been human if she hadn't been faintly alarmed.

Yet, following him into what was obviously his bedroom, she found herself able to give her surroundings the attention she'd craved. Once again the furnishings were spare but elegant, with carved antique cabinets at each side of the huge bed and a carved antique chest of drawers between the windows. Another door led into what appeared to be a dressing-room, with yet another bathroom beyond. The ceiling was high and richly carved, and a selection of misty water-colours adorned the walls. The whole ambience of the room was cool and understated, yet no one could pretend its simplicity was there by chance.

While Helen had been admiring the room's appointments Matthew had unlatched the long windows, and a draught of warm air swept into the room. It reminded Helen of how hot she'd been when she arrived here, and a hasty glance at her shorts and T-shirt showed her how right she was to feel apprehensive.

Matthew was obviously waiting for her, however, and, trying not to feel self-conscious about the way her clothes clung to her, she stepped past him on to the balcony.

The view was, as he had implied, magnificent. The curving arms of the headland were joined by the reef, and the ocean exposed its teeth with every surging tide. Right now the water was receding, laying bare the rocky promontory, and seabirds swooped unceasingly for the flotsam left by the tide.

'It's beautiful,' she said at last, aware that although the balcony didn't overlook the courtyard it was just a few yards away. The last thing she wanted was for Tricia—or Fleur—to look up and see her. It was going to be hard enough to explain her absence as it was.

The sound of Henry yelling his head off caused her to look beyond the courtyard, to where the pool was now in use. The party had evidently moved to the chairs on the poolside sun-deck, and Andrew must have found some shorts, because he was in the pool as well.

'I'll have to go,' Helen said with some consternation, realising she had already been longer than she'd thought. 'Can you imagine what—what Tricia will be thinking? I'm supposed to entertain the children; that's why I'm here.'

'No, it's not,' said Matthew quietly, easing her back into his bedroom and closing the windows. 'You're here because I invited you. Unfortunately, I had to invite the Sheridans also.'

Helen swallowed. 'Well, that's very—kind——'

'It's not kind at all, and you know it.' He was standing very close to her, just inside the windows, and she could feel the disturbing heat of his body. 'I wanted to see you again. Don't ask me why. I find you very attractive. Is that enough?'

Helen's legs seemed to have lost the ability to move. Which was silly, because he wasn't touching her, and she certainly wasn't frozen to the spot. On the contrary, she was sweating; an actual droplet of perspiration was trickling down her spine. Perhaps her legs were stuck together too, she thought. There had to be some reason why she didn't step away.

'I don't think——' she began, but his knuckles, tracing the line of her cheek before dipping beneath her jawline, silenced her.

'What don't you think?' he asked softly. 'That this is a good idea? Oh, it is, believe me.' His lips twisted. 'For me at least, it's imperative. Unless you want to drive me mad.'

Helen's breath escaped on a gasp. 'Mr Aitken——'

'Matthew.'

'Matthew, then.' She moistened her lips with a nervous tongue. 'Whatever you think—whatever impression I've given you by my behaviour—I'm not—I'm not used to—— Well, you know what I mean. I—I'm flattered, but I'm not interested. Now, please, I'd like to go back to the others.'

'Would you?'

His hand dropped to his side, but although he was no longer touching her she was as conscious of him as if he was. It was the way he was looking at her, she thought uncomfortably. As if he could see through her clothes, as if he could see through her *skin*. And, God help her,

her body was responding to him, without any volition on her part.

'Yes,' she managed finally, but, when at last she got her legs to move for her, his hand at her nape caused her to falter.

'You're hot,' he said, and she knew he must be feeling the line of wetness beneath her braid. 'Why don't you take a shower instead?'

'A shower!' The words were more of a squeak than anything else, but he didn't demur.

'Why not?' he asked gently. 'I find the idea—tantalising. There's something very sexy about a woman when she's wet.'

Helen stared at him. 'You're not serious!'

'Yes, I am.' His thumb invaded the neckline of her T-shirt and stroked softly over the fine bones that formed her shoulder. 'Your shirt and shorts are sticking to you. Despite the fact that you're obviously wearing a swimsuit. You can keep that on, if you like. I'll enjoy taking it off myself.'

Helen gulped. Then she shook her head. 'You're mad,' she said in a strangled voice. 'Absolutely mad!'

'Just aroused,' he corrected her huskily, pulling the loose neckline of the T-shirt off her shoulder. He bent his head and touched her bare shoulder with his tongue. 'So are you.'

'I am not.'

Helen's denial was as spurious as the hand she raised to stop him. In all honesty, she didn't understand what was happening to her, for, although she'd shared amorous interludes with men before, she had never felt the way Matthew made her feel. The lovemaking she'd experienced before had been strong on affection and weak on sex, but with Matthew she knew it would be different; when he touched her she started to burn.

'OK,' he conceded now, letting her have the way of it, but she sensed he didn't believe her any more than she believed herself. Why else would his hand reach for her, caressing her at her midriff, sliding beneath the hem of her shirt to spread his palm against her back?

'Mr Aitken—Matthew——' Her mouth was so dry she could scarcely get her tongue round it, and it didn't help when he moved nearer and rubbed his chest against her breasts. The hand she'd raised between them was crushed against hair-roughened muscles, and the fibres were surprisingly soft where they curled against her palm. 'We can't—*you* can't—do this.'

'Do what?' he taunted, looking down at her with sensual indulgence. 'What am I doing, for God's sake? Just inviting you to get cool. I can't help it if your puritan soul reads something more into my intentions. You are hot. I can feel it. And I think you can feel it, too.'

It was all double meanings and innuendo. For all her ignorance in some things, she wasn't unaware of what he really meant. Almost involuntarily, her eyes dipped to where his chest-hair arrowed beyond his navel. His brown flesh was smooth and masculine, his stomach taut and flat. But below his belt the fabric was taut, and her eyes tore away in panic.

'Please——' she begged, half aware that the solution was in her own hands. She had only to pull herself away from him, put the width of the room between them, and he wouldn't touch her again. Something told her she could stop him. Matthew Aitken didn't have to force himself on anyone.

'Please, what?' he asked, the tips of his fingers invading the waistband of her shorts now. The back of her swimsuit dipped low over her hips and he didn't have to push it aside to find the curve of her taut rear. Her muscles clenched instinctively as his finger found the damp cleft of her bottom, and a wet heat flooded between her legs as he urged her closer against him.

'Mmm, sweet,' he murmured huskily, his teeth fastening on to the skin of her shoulder and nipping the yielding flesh. 'You know what I want to do, don't you? It's not easy for a man to disguise his needs.'

His meaning was all too obvious. The way he was holding her was bringing her into intimate association with his body. And, although until that night on the beach she had had little experience of a man's arousal, there was no mistaking the solid feel of his sex pressed against her thigh.

Her breathing trembled. What she should do and what she shouldn't do were just abstracts, suspended in her brain. Thinking was becoming a problem; coherence was almost impossible. And, when he lifted his head and found her mouth, her sigh signalled her inevitable surrender.

His mouth was so sensual, slanting across hers first one way then the other, nibbling kisses at her lips until they were forced to part. Her hands, balled into fists, provided her only resistance. But when his tongue plunged into her mouth, every muscle felt suspended.

His hands cupped her buttocks now, lifting her against him. She could feel the whole length of him hard against her mound. His tongue performed a sensuous dance, miming what his body demanded. And, almost without volition, her hands crept to his neck, grasping handfuls of his hair, pulling him closer.

'God,' he groaned as she strained against him, her small breasts almost bursting out of her swimsuit. 'We are wearing far too many clothes. We've got to do something about it.'

'I don't want a shower,' protested Helen weakly, briefly sobered by his hands pushing her shorts down to her thighs.

'Well, not right now,' Matthew agreed, as her shorts puddled about her ankles. He lifted her legs about him and carried her to the bed. 'Maybe later, hmm?' he added, as she felt the coolness of the bedspread against her midriff. He tugged the T-shirt over her head and then frowned. 'What happened to the bikini?'

Helen caught her breath. 'I—it's too revealing,' she got out tremulously, and he uttered a lazy laugh.

'And this isn't?' he teased her softly, peeling the one-piece *maillot* down to her waist. 'Oh, God, Helen, let me touch you. I've been wanting to do this for days.'

Helen had the feeling that this was all some incredible dream. She couldn't be here, in Matthew Aitken's bedroom, letting him undress her without doing anything to stop him. She wasn't beautiful. She wasn't the kind of woman to drive a man mad with desire. As a matter of fact she was fairly ordinary—an awareness she'd felt even more strongly since she'd seen her mother again.

Matthew had shrugged off his shirt now, and, tugging her braid towards him, he went to work on her hair. In no time at all he had loosened the plait and drawn the sun-streaked strands over her breasts. Then, as she lay there, too dazed to feel embarrassed, he bent his head and took one erect nipple into his mouth.

The feeling that swept through her as he suckled on her breast was amazing. It was like an exquisite kind of pain that she didn't want to stop. It caused her to close her eyes, so that the sensual feelings filled her head. But when her lids flickered open, and she saw his bent head, the weakness she was feeling only intensified.

Dear God, she wondered, was this what it was like to want a man? Was the dampness between her thighs and the trembling in her legs a forerunner to what he meant to do to her? Knowing what happened was one thing; experiencing it was something else. Did she want this man to be the one to teach her, to show her how it could be?

She was in no state to decide, she thought, realising she was ducking the issue, but incapable of doing anything else. It had all happened too fast; she was still coming to terms with her own sexuality. And there was still that element of fantasy, of not believing that this was happening to her.

But it was. The heat of Matthew's body splayed beside her, his warmth, his passion, his smell—they were un-mistakable proof of what he was doing. For some incredible reason he wanted her, and her bemused senses couldn't handle anything else.

His mouth moved to her other breast, his teeth tugging an even greater response from her. She was weak, helpless, in the grip of emotions too strong to deny. Her pulse was racing, the blood rushing through her veins like liquid fire. She was on fire, she thought wildly. She was drenched in sensual flames.

When he drew her hand down to the bulge that swelled his jeans, she no longer tried to stop him. 'Help me,' he said. 'Touch me. Open the zip—that's right. Oh, God!' He caught his breath as she took hold of him. 'Oh, yes! Yes. That's so good.'

Helen's head swam. Was she really doing this? Was the living, throbbing thing in her hand a part of him? She knew it was. She could feel the blood beating beneath the sensitive skin, could feel his pulse racing against her palm. Hard and velvety smooth, it filled her with alarm as well as excitement. He was so big, so overpowering. And, although she was no foolish teenager, age did not necessarily bring reassurance in its wake.

Her fingers moved involuntarily, sliding up and down the length of him, so that he swore, quite explicitly, and removed her hand. 'If you do that, I can't be responsible for the consequences,' he told her thickly. Then, with unsteady fingers, he tugged her swimsuit down her legs.

She should have been embarrassed, and momentarily she did think of trying to cover herself. But somehow he'd managed to push his jeans away, and his hairy thigh came between her legs. Then he nudged the melting source of her femininity, and it was far too late to hide herself from him.

Her hips rose off the bed, almost in protest, but his fingers were already taking the place of his knee. They threaded between the moist curls, and she caught her breath instinctively. Then he rubbed the tiny nubbin hidden in the folds.

'Is that good?' he asked against her lips, as his tongue made another greedy foray into her mouth. His fingers moved again, sliding inside her, and a swelling sense of anticipation spread through her stomach and down her trembling legs.

'Don't—that is—I haven't——' she began chokingly, but the sudden eruption of her senses left her weak. A wave of shattering sweetness washed over her. She jerked against his fingers in helpless fervour as the feeling spread.

'Relax,' he breathed when she subsided again, but the shuddering that had gripped her body wouldn't stop. 'It was that good, hmm?' he added softly. 'You sure know how to drive a man insane.'

Then he was kneeling between her legs, his palms tantalising her breasts for a moment before dipping to draw her legs wider apart. His thumbs probed the soft creases, and she knew he was watching her reaction as he did it. But that didn't stop her bucking helplessly when he touched the place where he'd caressed her before.

She had to tell him, she thought dizzily, wondering if he was in the habit of making love to virgins. Or did he know? Had he guessed? For all he'd succeeded in arousing her, far beyond anything she'd imagined, surely he must know she was painfully ignorant of what came next?

But when his finger slid inside her again and found her wetness, the groan he uttered made it impossible for her to offer any last-minute confession. Besides, if she was honest with herself, she would admit that she didn't want to tell him. She didn't want him to think she was so inexperienced, so lacking in sex-appeal, that no man had touched her.

'God, Helen,' he muttered, as she lay there gazing at him with an unknowingly sensual invitation in her eyes. 'I wanted to make this last, but I don't think I can. There's a limit to my endurance, and I guess we just reached it.'

There was still time. As he reached towards the drawer in the cabinet beside the bed and pulled out a foil wrapper, Helen tried to find suitable words. But she saw what he was doing, and her mouth dried in helpless anticipation. He was protecting himself—and her. She had nothing to worry about. Nothing—nothing could go wrong.

How wrong she was.

His hands cupped her bottom, lifting her against him. The solid bluntness of his arousal was touching her now, there, in that place between her legs that suddenly seemed too small for what he expected it to do.

Yet he was still caressing her, his fintertips between her legs, holding her apart, drenching her in her own heat as she responded without volition.

And it was good. The feelings she had felt before flowered again as he caressed her, and when he pushed against her, her muscles expanded to meet him.

It was going to be all right, she thought, relaxing and letting her body receive him. She could feel him now, hard inside her, and her hips arched almost instinctively to meet his powerful thrust.

And then a sob escaped her. The pain was excruciating for a moment. Dear God, she hadn't dreamed it would hurt so much. All pleasure vanished as he pushed his way inside her.

'God!'

Matthew's exclamation was no less fervent than hers, but, although he looked down at her with hot, accusing eyes, there was no way he could prevent what was happening. Her cry, her sudden resistance, had caused her muscles to convulse around him, and the constriction was enough to send him shuddering into release.

He collapsed on to her, almost winding her with the weight of his heavy body. All the air exploded from her lungs in an unwary gasp and she lay there, gulping for breath, as his hips jerked helplessly against her.

CHAPTER TWELVE

BY THE time Matthew was capable of lifting his head, Helen was already beginning to move restlessly against him. Dismay, pure and simple, was mirrored on her expressive face; her eyes were bright with unshed tears, looking anywhere but at him.

And, curiously, it was her obvious distress that dispelled his own feelings of anger and accusation. Despite the undeniable relief he'd felt in slaking his own needs, his gratification had been tempered by the knowledge of what he'd done. Contrary to her belief, he was not in the habit of ravaging inexperienced women. And, if he'd known she was a virgin, he'd have probably let her go.

Or would he?

The point was moot, but no longer debatable. And, looking down into her drowned grey eyes, he wondered if he'd have found the strength to do anything differently. He'd wanted her—more, in fact, than he'd wanted any woman ever before. And, what was more, he still wanted her. He could feel himself growing hard at the prospect of doing it all again.

'Please...'

Her voice, soft and tremulous, nevertheless contained a note of recrimination. She was trying to get up, but his body wouldn't let her. She obviously wanted to get away from him, but he didn't want her to go.

Instead of complying with her wishes, Matthew lifted one hand and shaped the curve of her jawline. She jerked away from his touch, but she couldn't avoid it, and he allowed his thumb to invade the softness of her mouth.

'How old are you?' he asked suddenly, and she stopped struggling long enough to give him a wary look.

'Does it matter?'

He inclined his head. 'Humour me.'

She hesitated. 'Twenty-two.' Then, with some dignity, 'As—as you've got what you came for, can I get up?'

Her words irritated him more than a little, but he contained his anger and said quietly, 'So—how did you get to the age of twenty-two without—without——?'

He couldn't find the right words, but in the event he didn't need to. 'Just unlucky, I guess,' she responded, with obvious sarcasm, but he knew that she was hurting, and not just in a physical sense.

He sighed then. 'It's incredible.'

'Incredibly boring, don't you mean?' she retorted tightly. 'Perhaps I never had the opportunity. We're not all like—like that, you know.' He was fairly sure she'd been about to say 'Fleur', but she swallowed the distinction and gave him a guarded look. 'I'm sorry if I wasn't what you expected. If it's any consolation, you weren't what I expected either.'

Matthew traced the outline of her lower lip with his thumb. 'Is that your way of telling me you were disappointed?' he enquired gently, and her face suffused with scarlet colour.

'No!' she exclaimed hotly. And then, more steadily, 'You're only making fun of me again. Well, fine. The joke's on me. I should have had more sense than to stay.'

'I'm not making fun of you,' Matthew informed her evenly, his hand dipping into the hollow of her shoulder, before moving on down her arm. He could feel her trembling beneath his touch and he knew an inexplicable feeling of protection. Which was ridiculous in the circumstances, he thought. When he'd been the one to abuse her trust.

Needing to detain her now, as much for his own needs as hers, he added, 'Why did you? Stay, I mean? I would have let you go if you'd told me. I'd never have forced you, if that's what you believe.'

'I don't—that is——' His questing hand had found her breast, and a little shudder feathered her smooth flesh. 'I— don't know why I did,' she admitted honestly.

'Perhaps I was curious.' Her lips twisted ruefully. 'Someone—some *man*—had to do it.'

'And you chose me?'

'No. Yes.' She shook her head. 'I don't know.'

She was getting frustrated. He could sense it. Even though she refused to look directly at him, even though she refused to acknowledge how her own body was betraying her, a kind of raw panic was setting in. She was afraid of herself, he thought, with sudden intuition. She didn't understand her own needs. And, dammit, he'd done nothing to explain them to her. He'd just gone ahead and had his way.

Ignoring the protest of his own body, whose needs were all too understandable to him, Matthew levered himself up on his hands and withdrew from her. But when she would have rolled away, he grasped her shoulders. 'Wait,' he said, and something in his voice stilled her instinctive protest. 'I think it's time we took that shower. Come on, I'll show you where it is.'

She wanted to protest, he knew, but a glance at her inner thighs had her covering herself defensively, and, not giving her a chance to escape him, he swung her up into his arms.

The shower cubicle in the adjoining bathroom was plenty big enough for two, but she gazed at him in horror when he joined her. 'You can't,' she said, when he turned the taps on. 'I—my hair's going to get wet.'

'I'll dry it for you,' he replied softly. 'Now, stop making a fuss and enjoy it.'

He found himself in the unusual position of wanting to please her. When she reached for the soap he let her take it, even though his hands itched to do it himself. It was incredible, he could hardly keep his hands off her. And when he saw the water streaming off her breasts, and the upturned thrust of her nipples, he thought how frustrating it was to be good.

But at last she was finished, and, giving in to the urge he'd had all along to caress her wet skin, he pulled her back against him for a minute. 'Do you have any idea what you're doing to me?' he asked, nuzzling her shoulder. Then, with intimate enquiry, 'Do you feel better?'

Helen quivered, but he noticed she didn't pull away from him this time. 'I—I suppose so,' she said, squeezing her legs together when his fingers spread down her stomach. 'If—if you'll give me a towel, I'll get dried. I don't think my hair's very wet.'

'I'll do it,' said Matthew unevenly, letting her go with some reluctance. 'Step outside the cubicle. The towels are beside the bath.'

Forcing himself not to look at the way she curled in on herself in embarrassment, Matthew collected a huge bathsheet and wrapped it about her shoulders. 'Is this what you do with Sophie?' he asked, trying to distract her, but as he rubbed her trembling shoulders the towel slipped down to her waist.

Matthew's eyes sought hers then, and what he saw there had him reaching for her. She was nervous, no doubt, but she was also aware of his arousal. And he told himself that excused his disgraceful lack of control.

Gathering her up in his arms again, he carried her back to the bed, and although she whimpered something about her hair being wet he didn't respond to her plea. God, he thought, he'd never felt this way about any other woman. She was everything he wanted, and so much more.

It was strange, because usually he was such a restless animal. Once he'd had his way with a woman, he'd been glad to leave. And, apart from a couple of abortive affairs in his teens, he'd remained emotionally inviolate. He guessed Fleur's behaviour had something to do with it. Certainly he'd never trusted a woman since.

But suddenly this woman was making him feel emotions he'd considered were for mutts and school-kids. Ownership, the need for possession—he was aware he was feeling them both. Not to mention jealousy, he acknowledged tautly. The thought of some other man touching her drove him mad.

Her lips were pressed together when he touched them, but, as if the caressing brush of his tongue was all that was needed to break the spell, her jaw sagged almost instantly. The sweetness of her breath was like nectar in his nostrils, and, although he'd determined restraint, his tongue surged helplessly into her mouth.

Desire, hot and fluid, poured through his veins. And he wanted to pour himself into her just as urgently. Dear God, she was so sweet, so responsive, so passionate. He wanted her so badly, he didn't know how he was going to stop.

Then her hands crept up his chest, and he felt incredible. When they linked behind his neck and drew him closer, he felt as if he was actually on fire. The feel of her small breasts pushing against his chest was unbelievably erotic, and he tucked one hand between them to stroke her swollen core.

To his amazement, she didn't stop him. And, what was more, he could feel her musky arousal on his fingers. For some amazing reason she still wanted him. And his body ached to show her how it should be.

'You don't know what you do to me,' he got out unsteadily, and winced when her nails dug painfully into his shoulders.

'I—know what you do to me,' she whispered, and he realised what he'd hoped might be going to come true. She wound her arms around his neck. 'Do you think I might enjoy it more this time?'

'Depend on it,' he said huskily, parting her legs and bending to press his face against the damp cluster of honey-gold curls. 'Don't stop me,' he added, as she jerked a little nervously. 'Just let yourself go with the flow.'

Matthew remembered those words later, when he lay panting beside her. Lord, he thought, she was every man's dream come to life. Despite her inexperience, she'd responded without inhibition, and the pleasure he'd found with her had been intense.

In fact, he realised tautly, he'd never felt this way before either. Always, when he'd made love to a woman, there'd been some part of himself he'd held back. He'd found satiation, but not satisfaction; release but not relief. Yet, with Helen, he'd felt no sense of restriction. With her, he was a whole person; together, they were complete.

It was at once awesome and frightening. He'd never let anyone have that kind of control over him before. In many ways, he was an emotional virgin, he thought wryly. But, God, she made him eager to shed the shackles that state had wrought.

Realising he needed reassurance that he wasn't the only one who felt that way, he turned his head and looked at Helen. She was lying within the circle of the arm and leg he'd thrown possessively across her, but she seemed to sense his sensual appraisal because she slanted him a sleepy gaze.

'I can't stay here much longer,' she murmured ruefully, but he could hear the reluctance in her voice.

'I know,' he said, drawing a finger line from her breastbone to her navel. 'We've got to talk, I guess. And it's not easy to be rational in this position.'

'No.' Her lips parted, and for a moment she looked as anxious as she had done before. 'But was it——? I mean—it was all right, wasn't it? The second time, I mean. I didn't do anything wrong.'

Matthew's lips tilted lazily. 'You tell me.'

Helen licked her lips. 'It was—amazing. I didn't know—I didn't think—that is——'

His finger over her lips silenced her, and then he bent and replaced his finger with his mouth. 'I get the picture,' he said, when they were both deliciously breathless. 'We'll talk about that later. When the others have gone.'

'The others!'

Helen gazed at him with horror-stricken eyes, but Matthew wouldn't let her get away.

'I'm sure they've guessed what's going on,' he said flatly. And, at her anxious gasp, 'Does it matter? They're going to find out anyway.'

Helen swallowed. 'They are?'

'Aren't they?'

A twinge of her anxiety touched him then, but before she had time to formulate a reply the doors to the outer room were flung open and Fleur marched into the suite.

Matthew had never felt so furious—or so helpless—in his life. That Fleur should be here in his house was bad enough. That she should have the effrontery to burst into his private apartments unannounced was intolerable.

And short of confronting her—nude—there was no way he could throw her out again. An option that wasn't an option, in his present protective position.

Helen's reaction had been equally as violent, though he guessed she was more shocked than angry. Beneath his palm—the palm which moments before had been teasing the swollen bud of her breast—her heart was racing madly. And, although she hadn't a hope of dislodging him, her elbows were scrabbling for purchase on the pillows.

He wanted to wring Fleur's neck, he thought savagely. She had ruined his life once before, and he was damned if she was going to ruin it again. It was time he told her what he really thought of her. It was time to get her out of his life. She couldn't be allowed to embarrass Helen. Whatever happened, that was one thing of which he was sure.

But before he could speak, almost before he had had time to drag the silk sheet over their naked bodies, Fleur charged into the bedroom, with Lucas at her heels. Matthew guessed his assistant had come upstairs with Fleur to try and restrain her, but what he saw in the bedroom set him rocking back on his heels.

However, before Matthew could say anything in his own defence, before he could try and explain that this was not what it looked, Fleur screamed. Her cry, raw and anguished, echoed and re-echoed around the vaulted ceiling of the apartment. It caused Helen to jerk violently beneath him, and he soothed her pained expression with a kiss.

'Trust me,' he said, for her ears only, but she didn't seem to be listening to him any more. Her eyes were on the woman who had haunted him since his youth, and the anger he'd felt initially rekindled anew.

Deciding there was only one way to handle this, and that wasn't lying down, Matthew jack-knifed off the bed, taking the quilt with him. Then, wrapping it about himself, he faced Fleur with eyes that were as cold as glaciers. 'What the hell d'you think you're doing?' he snarled. 'Get out of here, before I throw you out myself.'

Lucas's face was haggard. 'I tried to stop her,' he said stiffly, as Fleur snatched a tissue from her sleeve and dabbed her eyes. 'I didn't know—I didn't think——' His expression mirrored his contempt. 'For God's sake, Matt, there are people downstairs! What are they supposed to think?'

'I don't give a damn what they think,' said Matthew harshly. 'Just get this mad woman out of here. I want her packed and out of my house.'

Fleur drew a dramatic breath. 'And can I take my daughter with me?' she enquired haughtily, drawing an anguished breath from Helen. Fleur threw the crumpled tissue on the floor. 'Oh, yes——' this as Matthew stared at her disbelievingly '—didn't she tell you she's my daughter? Why else do you think she came here, if not because of this?'

'That's not true!'

At last Helen spoke, and Matthew gathered the quilt about him as he turned to look at her. 'What's not true?' he found himself asking. 'You're not her daughter? Or—she—isn't why you came here? Why you let me take you to bed?'

Helen's face paled. 'I am her daughter——' she began, but he wouldn't let her finish. Like a house of cards, the world he'd been building for the two of them, ever since he'd realised how he felt about her, came tumbling about his ears. She was Fleur's daughter! The woman who for a few short minutes he'd thought he'd loved was the offspring of that vile creature. He couldn't believe it. He wouldn't believe it.

But he was very much afraid it was true...

CHAPTER THIRTEEN

'THERE's a letter for you, Miss Gregory.' Helen's landlady came out of her door as her tenant came running down the stairs. 'Couldn't climb all those stairs,' Mrs Reams added, patting her ample chest as if she was already breathless. And, as she weighed considerably more than her five-feet-two-inch-frame could support, Helen could quite understand her dilemma.

'That's all right, Mrs Reams,' she said now, taking the letter with barely a glance and tucking it into her trouser pocket. 'It's a lovely morning, isn't it?'

'Mmm.' Mrs Reams looked disappointed. 'Aren't you going to open your letter, dear? It might be something important.'

'I doubt it.'

Helen felt a fleeting twinge of sympathy for the garrulous old lady. Mrs Reams had probably examined the letter very thoroughly before handing it over. In the three months since Helen had been living in her top-floor bedsitter, she'd learned that Mrs Reams was extremely inquisitive. It frustrated her considerably that her tenant remained so obstinately close-mouthed.

'Well——' Mrs Reams gave it one last shot '—it's not one of those advertising circulars. I'd say it was from a woman. Your mother, perhaps?' she queried. 'Or your sister?'

'I don't have a sister,' replied Helen dampeningly. 'And I've really got to go. I've got a class in half an hour, and I can't afford to miss it.'

Mrs Reams adopted a resigned face. 'Oh, very well,' she muttered, turning back into her ground-floor apartment. It was obvious she was getting nowhere, and she was missing her game-show on the telly.

Meanwhile, Helen jogged determinedly towards the bus stop. She hadn't been lying when she'd said she had a class at half-past nine. She was taking an intensive course in word-processing and other secretarial skills, and she'd already learned that missing a class was to her disadvantage, not theirs.

But at least she was doing something positive with her life at last, she thought firmly. And a six-month secretarial course was all she could afford right now. She would have preferred to work with children, but that would have entailed a lengthy course at college. And the money she'd saved wouldn't last that long.

Still, the prospect of becoming a secretary was much preferable to working at a filling station. And she'd be supporting herself for the first time in her life. When she'd worked for Tricia, she'd always felt indebted to her. Now she was making her own decisions, and the outcome was up to her.

The bus arrived, on time for once, and after paying her fare Helen found a seat and dumped her haversack beside her. It was only then that she extracted the letter from her pocket. She couldn't delay reading it any longer, however fruitless the exercise might be.

It was from Tricia. She'd seen that at once, as soon as Mrs Reams had handed it to her. Her erstwhile employer had written to her twice since she'd terminated Helen's employment: once to convey her feelings, and once to send her a cheque.

In consequence, she couldn't possibly imagine what Tricia might want now. She'd made her feelings plain enough, and she'd sent her final salary. There didn't seem much else to say, unless Andrew had been causing trouble again.

Slitting the envelope, she extracted the thin sheet of writing-paper. It was a handwritten note, short and to the point.

Helen,
I've been contacted by Matthew Aitken's father. He'd

like you to get in touch with him. His address is given
below.
Tricia Sheridan.

Helen swallowed, and folded the slip of paper back
into the envelope. Then, turning her attention to the
window, she stared resolutely at the street outside. They
were passing a park, and she could see children with
their mothers. There were dogs, too, and an old man
rummaging in a bin.

What was he looking for? she wondered, noticing that
his clothes were fairly clean. Perhaps he was looking for
something he'd lost, she reflected grimly. She'd lost
something, too, but it wasn't something she was likely
to find.

The letter was still in her hands and, forcing herself
to act normally, she folded the envelope in half and
stuffed it back into her jeans. When she found a bin
she'd dispose of it, she told herself. If she left it on the
bus, someone might return it to her.

The secretarial college was the next stop, and, hefting
her bag, she got to her feet and made her way to the
front of the bus. 'Lovely morning,' remarked the driver,
responding to the slim young woman with her chunky
braid of hair. 'Too nice for working, eh? How'd you
fancy going for a spin on my bike?'

'No, thanks.'

Helen's smile was distracted, and, as if realising he
was wasting his time, the driver stood on the brakes with
a heavier foot than was necessary. 'Ooh, sorry, love,' he
said, as Helen was thrown against the handrail, but she
knew it had been deliberate.

'It doesn't matter,' she said disparagingly, and sauntered down the steps.

But once the bus had pulled away her defiance left
her, and Joanne Chalmers, a young woman she had
become friends with in the six weeks they had been
sharing the course, came to meet her with anxious eyes.
Joanne was the same age as herself, but she was already

married with a family. In consequence, she mothered all the girls and Helen in particular.

'Hi,' she said, falling into step beside her. 'What's wrong?'

'Oh——' Helen looked at her a little defensively. 'Um—nothing. Not really.' Then, realising Joanne would expect an explanation, she added, 'The driver was a bit fresh, that's all. He nearly tipped me off the bus.'

'Men!' Joanne pulled a sympathetic face. 'Aren't they just the limit! Barry and me had a bit of a barney this morning. Lindsey's got a rash, and he thinks I should take her to the doctor's.'

'Oh, dear.'

It was a relief to think about something other than her own problems, and Helen listened while her friend extolled the virtues of being single. 'I should never have had a baby at seventeen,' she said. 'My mother was right, only I wouldn't listen.' She grimaced. 'Mothers usually are right, aren't they? Oh—sorry. I forgot yours had done a bunk.'

Helen shook her head and turned away, in no state to think about Fleur at present. The letter from Tricia— and its connotations with Matthew—had resurrected the whole sorry mess, and she was unutterably relieved when a group of their fellow students came to join them and she had time to regain her composure.

Joanne probably thought mentioning her mother had upset her, Helen reflected ruefully, feeling the other woman's eyes watching her with some compassion. She'd told Joanne her father was dead, and that her mother had left them when she was a baby. It was the truth, if somewhat encapsulated, and it had prevented a lot of unnecessary questions.

Now, however, she found herself wondering what Joanne would say if she was completely honest with her; if she told her friend that her mother had accused her of seducing the man she loved. And what if she added the rider that the man in question had believed her, that he'd actually thought she'd done it to avenge her father's death?

Oh, God, she thought later that morning, as she stared blankly at the keys of the word-processor, she'd believed she'd got over it—or over the worst, at least. But the pain was no less acute because she'd been ignoring it for so long. On the contrary, it felt as if it had festered and infected her whole body.

She couldn't eat any lunch and, reassuring Joanne that she was just feeling under the weather, she decided to skip the afternoon's classes and spend the time in the park. She could have gone back to her bed-sitter, but Mrs Reams was bound to be curious, and she didn't want her asking questions that she wasn't prepared to answer.

It was a warm June afternoon and, finding an empty bench, Helen folded up her sweater and stuffed it into her haversack. The heat was pleasant on her bare arms, now exposed by the cotton vest she was wearing, and she tilted her head wearily and turned her face to the sun.

But the warm day was too reminiscent of that other warm day she had spent at Dragon Bay, and although she'd planned to throw the letter away she pulled it out of her pocket. The folds she had made bisected the paper; it would be incredibly easy to destroy. She should tear it into little pieces, she thought, and drop it into the nearest rubbish bin.

Instead, she extracted the slip of paper from its envelope again, and smoothed the creases out on her knee. The words were the same; Tricia was evidently still at odds with her. But this time she read beyond her signature; this time she read the address.

'Ryan's Bend,' she mused aloud, after taking note of the fact that apparently it was a stud farm. 'Benjamin Aitken, Ryan's Bend, Kinsville, Tallahassee, Florida.'

There was a telephone number, too, and Helen thought that if she had intended to contact Matthew's father, that was how she'd have done it. But, as she didn't intend

to contact him, as she had no wish for another verbal
bludgeoning, there wasn't much point in noting it down.

She sighed. She was surprised Tricia had agreed to
convey the message to her. Since the events of that
morning at Dragon Bay, Tricia had scarcely spoken to
her at all. It had been Andrew who had informed her
her services were no longer required, Andrew who had
contemptuously dismissed her anxious attempts to
explain.

'I always thought you were a sly minx,' he'd said, after
they were back at the Parrishs' villa. 'Butter wouldn't
melt, and all that. But you were holding out for richer
game.'

Of course, Tricia hadn't been around when he'd said
that. Or she might conceivably have wondered what he'd
meant. No, Tricia had retired to bed with a headache.
And Helen had borne the brunt of Andrew's temper.

She had wondered afterwards whether Tricia might
not have found it in her heart to overlook what had happened if Andrew hadn't put his spoke in. After all, her
work hadn't suffered. And the children liked to be with
her as well. But Andrew had insisted that they couldn't
continue to employ her; that she might be a bad in-
fluence on Henry and Sophie. And although in her
stronger moments Helen had known that he was jealous,
she'd despised herself so bitterly that she'd packed her
bags.

One of the worst aspects of the whole affair was the
suspicion she had that she'd proved to be no better than
her mother. After all these years of despising Fleur for
abandoning her home and family, it had only taken a
couple of weeks for Matthew Aitken to get her into his
bed. How had it happened? When she'd gone to Dragon
Bay that morning, she'd had no inkling of how it would
end. Even now, with the knowledge of that self-betrayal
behind her, she found it difficult to accept what she had
done.

And yet, if she was honest, she had to admit that at
no time had Matthew ever forced her to stay. True, he'd

kissed her, and caressed her, but he hadn't tied her down. She could have left at any time. She had had only to open the door. But somehow he had bewitched her, and she hadn't wanted to leave.

But why?

Three toddlers were playing ball under the protective eye of their parents, and Helen watched them, too, trying to put all thoughts of Matthew Aitken out of her mind. But although the children were beguiling, and so trusting in their innocence, she couldn't forget Matthew's face when Fleur had accused her of using him.

Fleur...

Helen's hands clenched together in her lap. She hadn't heard a word from Fleur since she had left the villa that morning. Her mother hadn't even tried to contact her and demand an explanation. It was as if she didn't exist, as if their brief reunion on the island had never happened. She knew now that Fleur had only been using her to ensure that her identity was never revealed.

The fact that Fleur herself had revealed it was immaterial now. Obviously, the shock of finding Helen and Matthew together had temporarily unhinged her mind. The way she'd looked, the bitter fury in her gaze when she'd seen her daughter, was forever imprinted in Helen's subconscious. That woman didn't love her. Helen thought she probably hated her now, for making her betray the truth.

A pain knifed through her stomach.

As always, it was the memory of Matthew that hurt the most. He had been so ready to believe Fleur; so ready to accuse her. It was as if he'd been expecting it; as if he'd wanted to believe the worst. And why? Had she just been a morning's diversion? He obviously hadn't cared about her feelings.

Not as she'd cared about him...

Helen frowned. Now where had that come from? She didn't care about him. She *couldn't* care about him. He was Chase Aitken's brother. The brother of the man who'd destroyed her father's life.

And yet...

Pulling out a tissue, she quickly blew her nose. She must be getting a cold, she thought tautly. Maybe that was why she was feeling so down. It wasn't the letter, or the weight of memory that came with it. It was just a dose of summer flu that was going around.

Her eyes watered suddenly and, scrubbing the heels of her hands across them, she felt an overwhelming sense of desolation. Who was she kidding? she chided herself painfully. Of course she'd cared about Matthew. That was why she'd been so desperate, why she'd tried to contact him again before she left.

She cringed now, thinking of that phone call. She'd been at the airport, waiting for the evening flight to London, and she'd been half afraid his number would be unavailable. But it hadn't been. The operator had given it to her directly. And she'd dialled Dragon Bay with trembling fingers, praying that Matthew would be there.

She'd wanted to explain, she'd told herself. Fleur had had her say, but Helen had been too stunned to defend herself. Besides, with Lucas there it had seemed such a fiasco. And Matthew had left her to it. He hadn't even said goodbye.

Lucas had answered the call, she remembered now. And, when she'd first heard his voice, she'd believed she was in luck. Lucas knew her; he knew she wasn't capable of the things her mother had accused her of. He'd understand why she wanted to speak to Matthew. He'd be on her side.

But he hadn't been. As soon as he had realised who it was, his voice, his manner, his whole attitude had changed. Matthew wouldn't speak to her, he'd informed her coldly. Matthew wasn't speaking to anyone. And he'd particularly mentioned her. He didn't want to speak to her again.

She'd hung up with a feeling of total annihilation. She'd boarded the plane to London and spent the whole trip in a daze. What she was going to do, where she was going to live—those problems hadn't touched her. It wasn't until she landed in England that she'd realised what she had to face.

Fortunately, the cold air of a March morning had helped to clear her head, and by the time the airport shuttle dropped her at Victoria she had a little idea of what she had to do. A bed and breakfast to begin with; and then somewhere more permanent to settle down; and a job—not necessarily in that order. She would never again rely on so-called friends.

In the event she hadn't found a job, but she had enrolled at the secretarial college. Six weeks of looking for work, and of spending her nights crying for something she could never have, had given her a new perspective on her future. She was alone, yes, but that didn't mean she had to take any employment that was offered to her. She had a little money saved and, if she was careful, she could take the secretarial course. Good secretaries were paid accordingly, and she intended to be very good.

But now this, she fretted, looking at the letter again. Why couldn't they leave her alone? Hadn't they done enough? Besides which, she hardly knew Matthew's father. She'd only met him briefly that one time. Which brought her thoughts round full-circle. Oh, God, why hadn't she destroyed the letter straight away?

She sniffed, feeling a burning behind her eyes that had nothing to do with influenza. She felt as if she'd been nursing an injury and now someone had exposed it, tearing aside the fragile skin that had been growing over the wound.

She read Ben Aitken's address again. A stud farm, she thought, trying to drum up the resentment she knew she should be feeling. No doubt that was where Chase Aitken had got his polo ponies. Did Matthew play polo as well?

No, she reminded herself, he was a writer. Since coming back to England, she'd learned he was a fairly successful one as well. She'd even borrowed one of his books from the library, but she hadn't been able to read

it. The words were far too close to him, and she'd severed
even that connection.

Stuffing the letter into her pocket again, she hoisted
her haversack and got to her feet. Sooner or later they'd
realise that she wanted nothing more to do with them.

The next few days weren't easy, but, like with everything
else, time put a welcome buffer between her actions and
her thoughts. She was busy with the course, and she even
had supper with Joanne and her family one evening. She
was making a life, she told herself. She didn't need anything—or anyone—else.

Then, one evening, when she got back from college,
Mrs Reams came to meet her with a conspiratorial smile.
'You've had a visitor, Miss Gregory,' she exclaimed confidingly. 'A gentleman. I said he could stay with me until
you got in, but he didn't want to. He said he'd come
back later.' She frowned. 'Are you all right?'

Helen felt limp, her legs like jelly. 'A gentleman?' she
echoed, not having got past that initial announcement,
and Mrs Reams nodded, giving her an anxious look.

'That's right, dear. An American gentleman, he was.
Not young, you understand, but ever so handsome.
Treated me like a lady, he did. He said he didn't want
to trouble me. Well, of course, I said it was no trouble
at all, but he still insisted he wouldn't wait.'

Helen let out her breath on a trembling sigh. 'He's
coming back?' she swallowed. 'When?'

'I don't know, dear. Tonight, I expect. I said you were
usually at home. I told him you were studying to be a
secretary.'

'Is there anything you didn't tell him?' asked Helen
sharply, and then felt sorry when Mrs Reams looked
taken aback. 'Oh—it doesn't matter. I'm just feeling
tetchy.' She hesitated. 'Did he give you his name?'

'His name!' Easily reassured, Mrs Reams gave a girlish
laugh. 'Oh, my, yes, aren't I silly? He told me his name
was Aitken. He said you'd know who he was.'

Helen's head sagged. 'Thank you.'

'You do know who he is, then?' the landlady persisted, and Helen gave her a rueful look.

'Yes. He's—a friend of my previous employer. I expect he's visiting London on business, and decided to look me up.'

It was a poor excuse, but Mrs Reams didn't seem to notice it. 'Your previous employer?' she said chattily. 'And who would that be, dear? I didn't realise you'd been working. I thought you said you couldn't find a job.'

'I couldn't. That is—— Oh, it's a long story.' Helen didn't want to get into that right now. 'Um—well, if he comes back, I suppose I'd better see him. Will you send him up, Mrs Reams? I shan't be going out.'

However, later that evening, Helen had cause to regret her rash words. Seven o'clock passed, then eight, with no sign of Matthew's father. If he had been going to come back, surely he'd have been here by now. Instead of which she was sitting here like a pigeon, just waiting to be knocked off its perch.

Apprehension set in, and a not-unexpected feeling of panic. Why was he coming to see her? she wondered. To confirm she'd got his message? And, if so, what had that message meant? Surely Fleur hadn't sent him, not after the way she'd behaved. And if she had, Helen didn't think she wanted to know.

And then, at about half-past nine, when she was thinking of getting ready for bed, there was a knock at her door. Her mouth dried, and her tongue felt as if it was glued to the roof of her mouth, but she had to answer it. She'd told Mrs Reams to send her visitor up. And the landlady knew she hadn't gone out.

For all her complaints that climbing the stairs was bad for her, Mrs Reams was standing beside the man waiting outside. It was Matthew's father, Helen saw instantly. And the tiny hope she'd nurtured, that Matthew might be with him, died a death.

'Here we are,' said Mrs Reams triumphantly, and Helen guessed her curiosity had got the better of her.

The landlady evidently wanted to see for herself how Helen would greet him, and when Ben Aitken held out his hand she was obviously disappointed.

'Sorry to be so late,' he said apologetically. 'I'm afraid I went back to my hotel and fell asleep. I flew over last night and I never can sleep on aircraft. Too much noise and turbulence. I hope you'll forgive me.'

So polite!

To Helen, who didn't quite know what she had expected, but certainly not such courtesy, his words were like a balm. Unexpectedly, she felt that awful pricking behind her eyes again. Turning away, so he shouldn't see it, she said, 'Please, come in.'

'I'll leave you, then,' said Mrs Reams regretfully. She turned to the man. 'It's good for Miss Gregory to have some company for a change. Quite a recluse, she is usually. Hardly goes out at all, and I should know.'

'Thank you, Mrs Reams.' Helen recovered sufficiently to give the landlady a reproving look, and the old lady pulled a face before starting down the stairs. 'I'm sorry,' said Helen, closing the door, 'I'm afraid Mrs Reams is rather nosy. But she means well, and she's been very kind to me.'

Ben Aitken stood just inside the door, looking politely round the room. Seeing it with his eyes, Helen was instantly aware of its shortcomings, but it was clean and neat and serviceable, and it was her home.

'Won't you sit down?' she asked, pointing to one of a pair of worn plush armchairs and moving towards the electric ring. 'Can I get you a drink? Some coffee, perhaps? I'm afraid I don't have anything cold.'

'Nothing for the moment,' replied Matthew's father easily, lowering his long length into the chair she'd indicated. He looked round again. 'So this is where you live. Mrs Reams told me you're studying at college.'

'Just secretarial college,' said Helen quickly, taking the armchair opposite and folding her hands in her lap. 'I—don't have any formal qualifications, you see, so I——'

'I'm not here to question what you choose to do with your life,' he declared at once. 'Just to—ensure that you're all right. We—— That is—my son—was afraid Fleur might make things difficult for you.'

Helen swallowed. 'Fleur?' she echoed faintly, and Ben Aitken nodded.

'You have seen your mother, haven't you?'

Helen shook her head.

'But she—we——' He was obviously finding this as awkward as she was, because he looped his hands over the arms of the chair and fixed her with a troubled stare. 'You haven't seen your mother? She hasn't been in touch with you at all?' He sighed. 'Oh, dear, Matt was right. She is only interested in herself.'

Helen took a breath. 'If—if it's any consolation to you, I don't mind. Not seeing her, I mean. I—we have nothing in common, whatever you believe. I thought we might have for a while, but I was wrong.'

'Even so——' Matthew's father looked uncomfortable. 'She was—supposed to come and see you. To make sure that you were all right. Matt knew you'd lost your job because of him, and he was anxious. He wanted to offer some—recompense.' He coloured. 'It was the only thing he could think of to do.'

'Matt!' Helen stared at him, aghast. 'You mean, Matt asked my mother to offer money to me? Ugh!' Her revulsion was obvious, and she sprang to her feet with distaste. 'I think you'd better go, Mr Aitken. I appreciate that this isn't your problem, but I've heard enough.'

Ben Aitken sighed. 'Miss Gregory—Helen—please——'

'No, I don't want to hear your excuses,' she told him stiffly. 'I know you thought what you were doing was right. But people do things differently on this side of the Atlantic. And if your son thinks he can buy——'

'He doesn't,' interrupted Ben Aitken heavily. 'Darn it, I knew I'd go about this the wrong way. Matt isn't trying to—buy—anything, Miss Gregory. He just wants to know you're—secure.'

'Why?' Helen's lip curled, and Ben Aitken looked up at her with rueful eyes.

'I would have thought that was obvious,' he said. 'He's concerned about you. He thought Fleur wasn't to be trusted, and it appears she wasn't.'

'So he thought he'd get you to offer me money instead.' Helen trembled. 'I find that insulting.'

'Do you?' Ben Aitken pulled a wry face. 'Well, where I come from they say pride doesn't put butter on your greens.'

Helen flushed. 'Well, you can tell—your son—I manage. Even if I didn't, I'd still want nothing from him.'

'Yes, I think he knows that,' affirmed Ben wearily. 'When you didn't answer his letters, he surely knew. But that doesn't stop him worrying about you, let me tell you. Goddammit, the man's hurting! Why else d'you think I agreed to come?'

CHAPTER FOURTEEN

HELEN sagged against the back of the chair. 'What did you say?' she asked weakly, and Matthew's father gave her an impatient look.

'Ah, hell!' he exclaimed. 'Matt'd kill me if he knew what I'd just said. Look here, Miss Gregory, I want you to forget it. It's not even relevant to why I've come.'

'It is.' Helen stared at him intently and then hauled herself round the chair and into the seat. 'What was that you said about—about letters? I haven't had any letters. Well, not from—from Matt, anyway. Just from Tricia.'

'Tricia?'

Ben looked confused, and Helen quickly explained that she meant Mrs Sheridan. 'The only communication I've received from the United States was when she sent me your address.'

Matthew's father frowned. 'But—Matt wrote to you. Twice, that I know of. It must be—two or three months ago now. Before he and Luke had that bust-up. Oh—you won't know—Luke has left.'

Helen blinked. 'Lucas doesn't work for Matthew any more?'

'No.' Ben looked rueful for a moment. 'Oh—you probably know—the guy was infatuated with you. Finding you with Matt that time—well, I guess it blew his mind. At any rate, he and Matt had the most god-awful row a couple weeks afterwards.' He grimaced. 'Wrecked the office, they did. Chucked his goddamn computer on the floor.'

Helen gasped. 'Matt?'

'What? No—Luke did it. I think it was aimed at Matt, but, thank God, he missed.' He gave a short laugh. 'That would have given Matt more than a mild concussion.

As it was, I had to fly down and help Ruth put things straight.'

Helen swallowed. 'You're saying Matt had a concussion?'

'Just a mild one,' said Ben drily. 'And you should have seen Luke's face. No——' he grimaced '—Luke didn't brain him; he hit his head on the metal cabinet. But it knocked him out, and Luke decided to get out while he still could.'

Helen shook her head. 'I don't understand.'

'Don't you?' Ben snorted. 'Well, I'm beginning to. Matt must have given those letters to Luke to post, and my guess is he didn't do it. I can't prove it, of course, but it makes sense. I think Luke would have done anything to keep you two apart.'

Helen tried to absorb what he was saying, but after all these weeks she'd given up on ever hearing from Matthew again. And even now she didn't really know what his father was doing here. What did he mean, Matthew was hurting? He couldn't mean because of her—could he?

And then another thought struck her. 'The day—the day I left, I tried to ring Matt,' she said carefully. 'Lucas—Lucas answered the phone, and he said Matt—Matt didn't want to speak to me.' She licked her lips. 'Do you—do you think he was lying? I never got a chance to explain, you see.'

Ben sighed again. 'This would be the day after—well, the day after you and Matt——' He broke off significantly. 'I don't know. I suspect he might have been telling the truth.' And when Helen's lips parted in consternation he added hurriedly, 'No one could speak to Matt for several days after that.'

Helen tried to be casual. 'Oh? Why?'

'Because——' Ben grimaced. 'Because he went on quite a bender. He took it hard, you see, you being Fleur's daughter. I guess he didn't tell you, but that woman blighted his young life.'

Helen's voice was barely audible. 'How?'

'Oh, you don't want to know.'

'I do want to know,' insisted Helen tautly. 'Please, I have a right to know. She is my mother, after all.'

'Which is why—— Oh, what the hell?' Ben lay back in his chair and gazed wearily into her face. 'When Matt was twenty-two, she tried to seduce him. And he's blamed himself for it ever since.'

Helen's breath caught in her throat. 'But—she was married to his brother.'

'I know.'

'Well—where was he when—when this was going on?'

'Nothing went on,' Ben informed her flatly. 'And Chase was away at the time. He often was.'

Helen hesitated. 'But—how do you know it was—it was like Matt says? Perhaps he——'

'Because it happened to me, too,' snarled Ben with sudden anger. 'Goddammit, what do I have to say? The woman's psychologically sick!'

Helen felt sick, too. 'I didn't know.'

'How could you?' Ben sighed. 'She's not your problem. But why do you think Chase had been drinking before that fatal match? Because he'd found her with some other man the night before.'

Helen trembled. 'And—Matt knows this?'

'He does now.'

'What do you mean?'

'I mean, I told him. As soon as I could talk some sense into him. I guess it was a couple of days after you left. I told him he couldn't believe a word she said.'

Helen moved her head. 'And he—believed you?'

'You mean, is that why he wrote to you? Yeah, I guess that sounds about right. But by then I think he'd come to the conclusion that he wanted you, whatever.' He scowled. 'I've never seen him in such a state before.'

Helen pressed her damp palms to her knees. 'I—don't think I understand.'

'Sure you do.' Ben sounded almost sardonic now. 'He sent me here because he believes you never want to see him again. He wouldn't listen to your explanation, so why should you listen to his?'

'I see you haven't eaten your lunch again,' Ruth chided her employer reprovingly. 'And that won't aid your digestion,' she added, nodding at the glass of whisky in his hand. 'I don't know what's the matter with you. You always used to like my cooking.'

'There's nothing wrong with your cooking, Ruth,' Matthew assured her evenly. 'The quiche was really delicious, and the apricot mousse just melted in the mouth.'

'But not your mouth, hmm?' Ruth observed wryly. 'Will you be working this afternoon, or shall I tell Vittorio he can have the afternoon off?'

Matthew scowled. 'What a trial you are, woman. No, I shan't be working. Tell Vittorio to come back tomorrow morning. I'll probably be working then.'

'Probably.'

Ruth went away, muttering to herself, and, leaving the table, Matthew carried his glass to the windows. The housekeeper could be a nuisance, but he knew she only had his best interests at heart. But the trouble was, he didn't have any enthusiasm for anything these days. He had more money than he needed, and his writing was too demanding in his present state.

He sighed, raising his glass to his lips and draining it in one gulp. Whisky, he thought. The total panacea. But unfortunately even that was losing its potency. In the last few days, he'd found nothing would dull the pain. Perhaps he should have taken his father's advice and gone to see her. But after what had happened—and the fact that she hadn't answered his letters—he'd chickened out.

All the same, he'd have thought the old man would have had a result by now. All he'd had to do was ring the Sheridans and get Helen's address from them. They couldn't know what Matthew had written in those letters.

But they must have had an address to forward them or they'd have sent them back.

But yesterday afternoon, when he'd phoned the hotel where his father was staying, Ben had been decidedly vague. He'd spoken to the Sheridans, he'd said, and yes, he had Helen's address. But she was staying somewhere out in the suburbs, and he hadn't had the energy to see her yet.

Naturally, Matthew had been concerned, but when—seizing the opportunity—he'd offered to fly over and join him, Ben had insisted that he stay where he was. He'd be all right, he said. He was only tired. But Matthew intended to ring again today, and if he was still feeling under the weather...

He looked down at his empty glass, and then turned back to where he had left the decanter. But although he removed the stopper he didn't pour any. Until Ben had spoken to Helen nothing was going to do any good.

The phone rang just then, and he practically lunged across the room to answer it before Vittorio could beat him to it. But then he remembered. He'd given Vittorio the afternoon off. His new assistant was a young Barbadian, and he lived in Bridgetown with his wife.

'Dad?' he exclaimed into the receiver, and then suppressed a savage curse when he heard his publisher's voice. 'Oh, hi, Marilyn. Yeah, I know, I did promise. But I did have a concussion, I told you that.'

Marilyn wasn't appeased. And Matthew guessed he couldn't blame her. The book was now three months overdue, and he was slacking. OK, he'd had his problems, but he was supposed to be a professional, for God's sake.

'Three weeks,' he said at last, having driven her up from the ten days she'd first suggested. 'Yeah, I'll deliver it myself. You have my word. I know, I've said that before, but this time I mean it. Just give me a few more days to get my head together.'

'It looks all right to me,' said a soft voice behind him, and Matthew swung round so sharply that the base of the phone went crashing to the floor.

He could hardly believe it: Helen was standing just inside the door. Then, as Marilyn protested, 'God—what? Oh, I'm sorry. I dropped the phone.'

She looked so good, he thought incredulously, hardly aware of what Marilyn said after that. A sleeveless green tunic, slit to the waist, over clinging white ankle-length leggings, gave her a sinuous, sensuous beauty. And her hair was loose for once, drawn back loosely at her nape with a white ribbon.

'Dammit, Matt, are you listening to me?'

Dragging his eyes from Helen's increasingly nervous gaze, Matthew knew he had to get rid of Marilyn without delay. Why Helen was here, what the old man had told her, were questions he needed answering. There was nothing more important. Whatever his publisher might think.

'Look, I've got to go,' he said, as Helen smoothed her palms against the panels of the door behind her. 'Um—something's come up. I can't talk now. Leave it with me, and I'll get back to you. Just don't hold your breath, eh, Marilyn? There are more important things in life.'

He saw the way Helen's expression changed when he mentioned the other woman's name and, drawing courage from that revelation, he said huskily, 'My publisher,' as he put down the phone. He swallowed. 'She's on my back because I haven't been doing any writing.' He shrugged. 'I guess I've had other things on my mind in recent weeks.'

'Like a concussion?' Helen suggested, proving his father had been talking, and Matthew felt a momentary anger towards the old man.

'It wasn't serious,' he said, with a taut grimace. 'I guess my skull's too thick to do it any real harm.'

'All head injuries are serious,' she retorted swiftly, and then, with a nervous twitch of her spine, 'I'm sorry. That is, I had no idea Lucas felt that way about me. I didn't give him any encouragement. I'm not like—like Fleur, whatever you think.'

Matthew conceded the point, suddenly aware that he hadn't shaved that morning, and that there was an unbecoming shadow of stubble on his jaw. The dining-room wasn't the place he'd have chosen to have this discussion either. But it was too hot outside, and he was loath to remind her of the last time she was here.

'Well, it's over now,' he said at last, when it became apparent that she had nothing more to say. 'Luke's gone back to working in television. I got a request for a reference from a news station in New York.'

'Oh.'

Helen nodded, and, realising he couldn't restrain himself any longer, Matthew decided to confront his fears right off. 'Yes,' he said, massaging the tense muscles at the back of his neck with unsteady fingers. 'Was—was that the only reason you came?'

Helen straightened then. 'Not exactly,' she replied, and Matthew felt a tightening in his loins. 'I came to—to tell you I—didn't get your letters. Your father said you'd written to me, but I didn't know.'

Matthew blinked. 'Son of a——' He broke off abruptly, and stared at her with uncomprehending eyes. 'But the Sheridans knew where you were living, didn't they?' He shook his head. 'They must have. How else did the old man get your address?'

'Oh, yes.' Helen moistened her lips with the tip of her tongue, and Matthew wondered if she had any idea how much he longed to feel that tongue in his mouth. 'Tricia had my address, and she wrote and told me that your father wanted me to contact him. But——' she coloured '—I thought it could only be because—because of what had happened. And, well—I didn't want to go through all that again.'

Matthew stared at her. 'Let me get this straight. You didn't get my letters, but you did get the message from my father?'

'Yes.'

'So what happened?' He scowled. 'If Sheridan held them back, I'll——'

'He didn't.' Helen hesitated. 'At least, your father and I don't think so. Mr Aitken said you probably gave them to Lucas to post, and—well, maybe—maybe he didn't.'

Matthew swore. 'So—when my father came to see you—I'm assuming he did come to see you—yesterday?'

'The day before.'

'Until then, you thought I still believed what Fleur had said?'

She nodded.

'Dear God!' He raked back his hair with an aggressive hand. 'And here was I, thinking you still hated my guts for what I'd done.'

Helen lifted her slim shoulders. 'I—never—hated your guts,' she told him softly, and Matthew felt some of the misery he'd been carrying around since she left lift from his shoulders. 'What happened—happened because I wanted it,' she went on carefully. She took a breath. 'Your father said you were worried about me. Does that mean you've forgiven me for who I am?'

'There was nothing to forgive,' said Matthew gruffly. He'd waited so long—without any hope of redemption—to hear her say those words, and even now he could scarcely believe she was here. 'I had no right to accuse you. My God, you're not your mother's keeper. And you were the best thing that had ever happened to me, besides.'

'Was I?' she asked faintly, and he uttered a sigh.

'Of course,' he said, 'but I guess that's why I found it so easy to believe the worst. What Fleur said—— God! It made a horrible kind of sense. And after what Chase had done to your father...' He shook his head.

'Oh, Matt!'

'I know, I know.' He gripped the back of his neck with painful fingers. 'But I'd never felt that way before, and I was hooked. Fleur and me—well, let's say she has reason to resent me.' He grimaced. 'I was one of her—disappointments, and she doesn't forget.'

Helen hesitated. 'I know.' Then, at his look of surprise, she added ruefully, 'Your father told me. He's worried about you, too, but I expect you know.' She shook her head. 'There's a lot of things I don't know about my mother. But I don't think I blame Chase any more for what happened to my father.'

Matthew's eyes narrowed. 'And me?' he said. 'What about me? Can you ever forgive me for treating you as I did? I should never have let you leave the island. I should have trusted you. You're nothing like Fleur, and I was a fool to let you go.'

Helen swallowed. 'It doesn't matter.'

'It does, too.' He took a step towards her and, stretching out one hand, he brushed the back of his knuckles against her cheek. 'Are you going to stay? Are you going to let me make it up to you? I never thought I'd be grateful to the Sheridans for anything, but I'm really glad they fired you right now.'

Helen stiffened. 'You don't have to feel responsible for me.'

'But I do.'

'No.' She dashed her hand across her cheek, as if to remove the imprint of his fingers. 'You don't understand. I didn't come here because I want you to—to help me. I've saved some money, and I'm taking a secretarial course so that I can get a decent job.'

Matthew closed his eyes for a moment. 'But I thought——'

'What did you think?' she demanded, suddenly distraught. 'That as soon as your father contacted me, I saw a meal-ticket for life?' She caught her breath. 'I'm not like that. I don't need your money. I've seen what money can do, and I'm not impressed.'

Matthew took another step towards her. 'And me?' he said. 'What about me? What if I need you? Doesn't that count?'

Helen shook her head. 'You don't need me.' She spread her hands. 'You don't need anyone. Besides, there are any number of beautiful women more than eager to do anything you say. I was just—a novelty. A silly virgin. But that doesn't mean you have to look after me for the rest of my life.'

Matthew drew a steadying breath. 'And what if I want to?' he asked. 'What if I tell you that's why I thought you'd come here? Because I thought you shared the way I feel? My father told you so much about me. Didn't he tell you I was crazy about you, too?'

He saw the tremulous hope dawning in her face and, taking advantage of her momentary uncertainty, he grasped her wrists and pulled her towards him.

'Didn't he tell you I love you?' he demanded, taking her arms behind his back and staring down into eyes grown misty with longing. 'I do, you know. That's why I was such a fool. I was afraid...'

'Afraid?' she whispered, and, realising he didn't have to imprison her any longer, Matthew cupped her face in his hands.

'Yeah, afraid,' he breathed, bestowing a kiss at the corner of her mouth. 'Afraid I'd made a mistake. Afraid you didn't feel the same way.'

Helen moved her head. 'But you knew——'

'What did I know?' he countered, running a line of kisses along her jawline before finding her mouth again. 'That I was the first man who'd touched you? That I'd taken advantage of your——?'

'Don't.' She raised her hand and pressed a finger against his lips. 'You didn't take advantage of me. I— I wanted you just as much as you wanted me.'

'And now?'

'Now?' She looked doubtful.

'How do you feel now? Are you going to put me out of my misery?'

'Oh, Matt.' He felt her hands slip beneath his shirt and spread damply against his spine. 'If—if you want me, I—I'm here.'

His eyes darkened. 'For how long?'

She coloured. 'I don't know what you mean.'

Matthew's thumbs brushed her lips. 'Are we talking weeks, here, or months—or a lifetime commitment?'

He felt her tremble. 'As—as long as you want me, I suppose.'

'That so?' His fingers slid into her hair. 'Well, Miss—Graham? Gregory? Whatever the hell your name is, you just got yourself a life-sentence.'

It was the evening of that day before they really talked again. Some time after sundown, Helen stirred in the silken comfort of Matthew's huge bed to find he had turned on the lamps and was watching her with a decidedly possessive smile on his dark face.

'You must have been tired,' he remarked, dipping his head and stroking her bare shoulder with his tongue. 'I like watching you sleep.'

Helen coloured, and groped for the sheet, but he wouldn't let her cover herself. 'Don't ever hide yourself from me,' he whispered huskily. 'You're beautiful, and I'm never going to get tired of looking at you.'

Helen relaxed. 'Nor I you,' she admitted sweetly. 'Oh, Matt, I do love you.'

'Do you?' A dark brow arched. 'I'm so glad to hear it.'

She frowned. 'What do you mean?'

'Well, you didn't say that before,' he told her drily. 'I hoped, but...'

'Matt!' She got up on her elbows and looked down into his lazy face. 'You knew how I felt. I—I just don't find it that easy to—to say what I feel.'

'No?' His hand cupped her nape, under the glorious tangle of her loosened hair. 'Well, let me see, what else can I do to help you?'

'You know what I mean,' she exclaimed hotly, and then, realising he was teasing her, she bent and nipped his lip with her teeth. 'Devil,' she said. 'You were never in any doubt.'

Matthew grinned. 'If I say I was, will you do that again?'

Helen shook her head. 'You're incorrigible.'

'Just insatiable,' he corrected her softly. 'For you.'

And for several minutes Helen couldn't answer him.

But when he eventually allowed her to prop herself above him again, she said, 'About Fleur——'

'To hell with Fleur,' he retorted feelingly. But at her troubled look he relented. 'The last we heard she was in Los Angeles. She'd apparently hooked up with some other poor guy.'

'No?'

'Yes.' He sighed. 'That was when I became convinced that she hadn't bothered to find out if you were OK.'

Helen grimaced. 'Well, I suppose that's something to thank her for,' she mused, but Matthew didn't look convinced.

'Mmm,' he said wryly. 'Well, at any rate, she shouldn't be bothering us again for some time. And once we've made her a grandmother, she's not going to find it easy to forgive us.'

Helen caught her breath. 'A grandmother,' she echoed, and Matthew drew her down to nuzzle her cheek.

'Well, maybe not immediately,' he said. 'There's the wedding to arrange first, and the honeymoon...'

Helen stared at him. 'Is that a proposal?'

'Unless you want me to get down on to my knees. I will, but not right now. You've tired me out.'

'You!' Helen punched his shoulder. 'I should refuse to accept it.'

'But you won't,' he teased, and then, with a trace of concern, 'Will you?'

'No,' she conceded ruefully, and with a triumphant groan Matthew rolled her on to her back and imprisoned her beneath him. 'Providing...'

'Providing?'

He stopped what he was doing to stare down at her, and she gave him a mischievous smile. 'Providing you'll ask your father to be your best man,' she finished, finding herself incapable of saying anything to burst his bubble of happiness, and he gave a hoot of laughter.

'Oh, yes,' he said, his thigh sliding between hers. 'My father will be more than willing to oblige. After all, someone's got to inherit Ryan's Bend, and he's been aching for a grandson for years.'

BRIDE'S
BAY RESORT

UNLOCK THE DOOR TO GREAT ROMANCE
AT BRIDE'S BAY RESORT

Join Harlequin's new across-the-lines series, set
in an exclusive hotel on an island off the coast of
South Carolina.

Seven of your favorite authors will bring you exciting stories
about fascinating heroes and heroines discovering love at
Bride's Bay Resort.

Look for these fabulous stories coming to a store near you
beginning in January 1996.

Harlequin American Romance #613 in January
Matchmaking Baby by Cathy Gillen Thacker

Harlequin Presents #1794 in February
Indiscretions by Robyn Donald

Harlequin Intrigue #362 in March
Love and Lies by Dawn Stewardson

Harlequin Romance #3404 in April
Make Believe Engagement by Day Leclaire

Harlequin Temptation #588 in May
Stranger in the Night by Roseanne Williams

Harlequin Superromance #695 in June
Married to a Stranger by Connie Bennett

Harlequin Historicals #324 in July
Dulcie's Gift by Ruth Langan

Visit Bride's Bay Resort each month wherever
Harlequin books are sold.

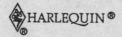

HARLEQUIN®

BBAYG

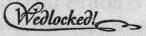